Spotlight On
Norman Firth

Volume Two

WILLIAMS & WHITING

Cover design by
Timo Schroeder

9781915887597

Williams & Whiting (Publishers)
15 Chestnut Grove, Hurstpierpoint,
West Sussex, BN6 9SS

CONTENTS

INTRODUCTION
THE RETURN OF NORMAN FIRTH
by **Philip Harbottle**

English writer Norman Firth was born on 8th October 1920, in Crupsall, Manchester, to Mary and Henry Wesley Firth. His first employment consisted of factory work, and during the early years of the war, he had aspirations to become a writer. His first short story was published under a pseudonym in 1940 and following his marriage in 1944 he became a full-time writer.

He was immediately successful, because he took full advantage of the peculiar British climate of "mushroom" publishing caused by wartime austerity, including paper shortages, which continued for several years after the war finished. Myriad small presses sprang up, hungry for all kinds of genre fiction, both adult and juvenile. Few, if any, of these publishers, strived for literary quality, nor did they pay royalties—only a flat fee.

Firth was a talented and compulsive writer, and was soon averaging 6,000 words a day, selling many short stories to magazines such as *Stag* and the myriad Gerald G. Swan publications, both adult and juvenile. In 1946 he was briefly an associate editor for the British magazine *Galaxy*, before publishing his own magazine *Gaze*, and gained a thorough grasp of writing markets. He adopted the byline of 'N. Wesley Firth', adding the middle name of his father to his own.

Like several talented British writers at that time, he decided on a policy of quantity over quality, finding that he could readily sell first-draft material to these small

1

publishers. After all, a mediocre first draft story paid the same fee as a well written one, and in the time taken to polish and revise a single story, another two or three first draft stories could be written and sold.

Firth was commissioned by many small publishers such as Bear Hudson, Curzon, Gerald G. Swan, Hamilton & Co., Mitre Press, Paget, John Spencer, and Utopian Publications to turn out lurid crime, western and science fiction stories. The stories were of all lengths, from short novel or novella length (ca. 30-40,000 words) to short stories of 2,000 to 20,000 word novelettes, and often published in "magazine" formats that changed their titles with each issue, in order to qualify for the maximum paper quotas. Where a 'magazine' contained all stories by one writer, that writer was obliged to create (or have foisted upon him by the publisher) a different pseudonym for each story.

Despite their speed of production, several of these novellas and novelettes were vividly exciting, where the author had evidently been seized by a really good idea.

Firth is only one of many writers obliged to work for the post-war UK "mushroom" publishers whose writing has received a bum rap from the critics and literati. His writing has been dismissed unread as dire hackwork and consigned to the literary dustbin, remaining out of print for over sixty years! But this dismissal was based entirely on only a dozen or so science fiction short stories comprising the infamous magazines, *Futuristic Stories* and *Strange Adventures* in 1947 (both had only two issues). Published with atrocious lurid juvenile artwork, and printed on shoddy quality post-war austerity pulp paper that was hard to read, they had been commissioned at impossibly short notice by one of his UK mushroom publishers, Hamilton & Co. Immediately on publication these were greeted with howls of derision and outrage, and since noted editor and critic Walter Gillings had earlier revealed Firth as being their sole author in his widely circulated *Science-Fantasy Review*, Firth's reputation in the science fiction world was blighted.

As a reader and collector, I myself was someone who went along with the accepted wisdom and ignored Firth. But when I was writing a book on post-war British SF, for the sake of completeness I was obliged to examine his only SF novel, *Terror Strikes!* (Hamilton & Co., 1946).

The atrociously poor paper (actually see-through) and tiny typeface made this impossible to read comfortably, so I was only able to skip-read it. My recorded lukewarm assessment was: "a routine reworking of Wells' *The Invisible Man*."

A major factor causing Firth to remain in obscurity for many years was the fact that a great deal of best work was hidden behind unknown pseudonyms and house names. This anonymity was a pernicious practice that was forced upon authors by many publishers in post-war Britain.

E.C. Tubb was a writer who also began his career in this post-war austerity publishing climate. In an interview, he told me: "I was a chap who was asked by publishing houses to produce books—or sometimes I went to them. They'd tell me that they'd pay so much, and some of them would offer a little more than the other chap. So you sat down, and did whatever you did as quickly as you could. Now, because publishers were nasty, and grasping and mean (they still are!) the advent of the house name came in. If someone became very popular, the publisher owned the house name, and that's where the nom de plumes started.

"With Curtis Warren you were 'King Lang', you were 'Karl Marx' or whatever—half a dozen authors all using the same name! These bylines were distinct from the *nom de plume* you deliberately chose because you had two stories in one issue of the magazine, so in that case you became 'Charles Grey' or somebody else. But the novels started that way, and then of course by the laws of the marketplace, you became that publisher's author, until somebody else wanted to use you and invented a different name. It became a kind of merry-go-round....

"...Looking back on my early days now, I can see that in the beginning, I was the pawn of the publisher. They said they would give you X pounds, and you took it, or you left it...and if you didn't, someone else would!"

Some of Firth's pseudonyms were known or suspected, since where his own name appeared in a 'collection', it was odds-on that the remaining stories were his. Known names Firth used include the earliest Earl Ellison stories (which later became a house name), Jackson Evans, Joel Johnson, and Leslie Halward, but so prolific was the author that many more remained undiscovered. Working with my collector colleague Morgan Wallace, I discovered several more by reading contemporary stories and recognizing his style, which was vastly superior to most of his fellow journeymen writers. The more of his work I uncovered, the more impressed I was, and I decided that it deserved to be returned to print...and published under his own name!

Late in 1947 Firth had accepted a lucrative commission from *Utopian Publications* owner Benson Herbert to write 30,000 words a month of "spicy" stories for his dubious line of men's magazines. As an added inducement Herbert offered accommodation for the author and his family—his wife and their young daughter, Sheila, who had been born in September 1945—in the basement of his home at Roland Gardens in London. For over a year, things went well. The prolific Firth was not only able to supply endless copy to Herbert, but with a basic income guaranteed from his "pulp" work, he was finally able to begin writing serious novels intended for better markets. But the arrangement was to have a tragic outcome. Sydney J. Bounds, another contemporary author, recalled to me in an interview that:

"He (Firth) wrote virtually the entire contents of the *Utopian* magazines, one after the other—until he suddenly went down with TB. This was a very serious disease in those days: there was no known cure. Within a matter of weeks, Firth had died, Benson had to act quickly to find a replacement. Since I'd done one or two stories for him, he hired me to supply 30,000 words a month."

The ailing Firth and his family moved back to his mother's house in Birkenhead, where he died on 13th December, 1949, with his family at his side. His mother was convinced that Firth had contracted the disease because of his frequenting of the "dusty damp old bookshops in little backstreets in London." He was only 29 but had published several million words. He continued writing right up to the end of his life, and managed to complete and sell his first full-length crime noir novel, *When Shall I Sleep Again?*

This was an extraordinarily good novel, intended for mainstream hardcover publication. It was picked up by John Gifford Ltd and published posthumously in 1950. Its quality ensured that it was quickly selected for republication by *The Thriller Book Club*.

Loosely based on James M. Cain's "noir" classic *The Postman Always Rings Twice*, this engrossing adult novel displayed for the first time the true potential of its author. Had he lived, Firth would undoubtedly have gone on to establish himself as a major talent with better publishers. His very last crime novel, *This Proud Castle*, was also a superior effort. It is one of the earliest detective murder mysteries to include homosexual elements, written when homosexuality was still illegal in the U.K. Completed just before he died, it was never submitted anywhere, but was retained by his wife until she died in 1997, when it passed to Sheila's stepsister.

Herself widowed at 32, Sheila had emigrated to Australia, and lived there for the rest of her life, after marrying Terry Ings in 1998.

The existence of Firth's unpublished novel might have remained unknown, until Morgan Wallace, researching Firth's work, discovered the existence on-line of some "new" short stories attributed to 'N. Wesley Firth'. He was finally able to establish that their author was actually Firth's daughter in Australia and managed to trace Sheila in 2012. Answering his letter, Sheila provided the valuable biographical information I have used in this article, together with family photographs. She told him:

"You were right about some of the short stories on the internet being written by me. I published three or four on a website called *Authors Den*. I also wrote a book, *Norman's War* under this name. Why I did this was that I always had this book in me, and it seemed appropriate to use dad's name.

"His unpublished manuscript is with my half-sister in the U.K. and she has been planning to send it to me for the past year. I will chase her."

Morgan Wallace brought *When Shall I Sleep Again?* to my attention as a literary agent in 2013 as a possible candidate for the *Linford Mystery Series*. On reading the copy he had sent me, I discovered that Firth was actually a talented writer. When Morgan told me of his exchange with Sheila and the existence of an "unpublished manuscript" I immediately wrote to Sheila myself. She readily agreed to be represented by my *Cosmos Literary Agency*, and thereafter we worked together to uncover and assemble the best of his work for publication in the *Linford Mystery Library*.

At my request, Sheila finally obtained from her half-sister the battered and fading unpublished manuscript and sent me a photocopy. It turned out to be a hitherto unknown murder-mystery novel. After I had laboriously retyped and edited it, retitling it *Murder at St. Marks*, it was immediately accepted when submitted to UK large print publisher F.A. Thorpe. I did the same thing with *Terror Strikes* (actually a first-class crime thriller with 'routine' SF trimmings) and this book was also subsequently reprinted by Endeavour Venture Press in 2019. They had earlier issued two of Firth's short novel Westerns in 2017, *Death at Catspaw Mountain* and *Guns of Calliope*. Many of his other Western novellas are set to be released as Ebooks by Wolfpack Publishing.

Sadly, Sheila Ings passed away in November 2018, at her final home in South Yunderup, Western Australia. But she had lived to see her father's work rediscovered and returned to print, thanks to her dedication to his memory, and was survived by her husband and two grown up children and her "five lovely grandchildren".

I have been pleased to assemble the best of Firth's crime fiction for republication in Williamson & Whiting's *Vintage Crime Library*, and all lovers and collectors of vintage detective fiction have a treat in store!

FIND THE LADY

CHAPTER 1

HOT LEAD FOR SPAGLIOTTI

The ringing of the phone by my bedside impinged on my eardrums with jarring discord. I blinked my way back to wakefulness and, under my breath, said some rude words.

After a hard day chasing the lowdown on a society divorce, and covering a baby show at the City Hall, I had looked forward to a peaceful night's sleep. But it wasn't to be, for a glance at the clock showed me it was only just one in the morning.

As I said, I'd worked hard for the paper all day, and later I had had some urgent and tedious business of my own to attend to. And now, after all that, there was that God-forsaken phone ringing. I picked it up, yawning, and barked into the mouthpiece:

"Anita Curzon speaking—who's calling?"

"Listen, Anita." I recognized the harsh voice of the night editor, Raymond Claxon. He sounded highly excited, as if something big had broken. He went on: "Anita, I'm in a spot! Like a fool, I sent all the boys out on assignments, minor things like fires, and prowlers—I know I shouldn't have let the lot go, but we were hard up for news, and I wanted anything that could be crammed in. I don't expect any of them back for at least an hour—and now there's really big news waiting to be picked up! Anita, you've always wanted to be a crime reporter, and so far you haven't had the least chance to prove you could handle that kind of assignment. But if you'll get out on this case I've got here, I'll see you're permanently assigned to crime. On top of that you'll be getting me out of a spot!"

I sat up interestedly. It's true I'd always had a yearning to handle murder jobs and such like, but Greason the day editor, had never given me a break. Now, apparently, here was a crime waiting for a reporter—and although so far I'd only handled scandal columns and minor shows of all types, here was my chance to show I could do something really big.

"I don't mind getting up for that, Mister Claxon," I told him. "Is it something really big?"

"Really big?" he echoed. "Why, it's the biggest thing that's broken since the Lindbergh snatch! The sooner you get over there the better, Anita. It's happened at the Graham Hotel; Mike Spagliotti was staying there, if you remember."

I remembered all right. Mike Spagliotti the craftiest, most brutal gang leader America had ever produced! Always too cunning to be caught out, but committing fresh crimes every hour of the day, through his precious gang. Yes, I remembered Spagliotti.

"What's Spagliotti got to do with it? Has he been up to some of his tricks?" I said carefully.

"No! And he never will be again, I guess. Mike Spagliotti was found half an hour ago with three bullets through his brain!"

I didn't feel so surprised. If the law couldn't execute Spagliotti, one of his enemies had been sure to, sooner or later.

I said: "How was it done? Have they found out anything?"

"How should I know? The desk clerk just freelanced the report in to us. I believe Detective-Inspector Flannel is on the spot already."

"Flannel? I've heard of him. He's the copper who's so darned hard on reporters, isn't he?"

"That's so—he hates 'em. But maybe you can do something with him—turn on the old charm, get me?"

I got him all right. And I didn't kid myself he was just flattering. Oh, no; I know I've got plenty of charm—and then some, and if you think I'm a little—or even a whole lot—conceited well, I can introduce you to about twenty men of all types who'll support Claxon's view.

I said: "I'll go right over. Thanks for the opportunity!"

"Swell!" he exclaimed "And say, Anita, regarding the opportunity: remember it isn't going to knock any more than once! If you muff this job, Greason'll see you never get another smell at crime stuff. So it's as much in your interests as mine to make something out of this! Shouldn't be hard. Big racketeers don't get eliminated every day of the week!"

I flopped the phone down, yawned and climbed out of bed with a prolonged shiver. No, it shouldn't be so hard to make something of it...

I looked in the mirror, was satisfied that I hadn't been in bed long enough to have spoiled my hairdo, or the make-up which I had been too tired to take off, after I got through with my business that evening.

I pulled my best nylons on, cast a critical eye over the seams where they ran straight and true up my long, slim legs. Fine. I got into my underskirt, and over it put on a smart costume of flecked brown. Then a brown swagger and a small, pert green hat, green bag and gloves and I was ready for the road...and if I failed to ogle Detective-Inspector Flannel I'd eat that green hat of mine.

I hadn't much trouble finding the Graham Hotel. In fact, the first taxi jockey I hailed knew where it was without any questions. Perhaps because of the fact that, although an expensive place, it literally was infested with big shots in the racketeering world. Here they paid high for apartments, the advantages being that all walls were bullet proof and sound proof.

The taxi decanted me on the pavement in front of the place, and I paid the driver and entered. There was a thin, very pasty-looking youth at the desk, and as I came in, he whistled loudly.

"Cut out the howling, wolf," I smiled, "and tell me where I'll find the corpse!"

"You know the deceased?" he asked in surprise.

I let him get a glimpse of my press card, and he nodded.

"You're a bit late, Miss Curzon," he told me, having seen the name on the pass. "The boys from the other papers have been here half an hour—but you don't need to worry— Inspector Flannel won't permit any of them to see the body yet, and he ain't given out any statement. They're all waiting outside Spagliotti's suite. You can head right up."

I thanked him with a smile which had him rocking on his stool, and as I went up in the lift I knew his eyes were busy peering after my legs. I didn't mind that; I know men like to see a nice pair of legs, and I'm only too glad I have a nice pair to show them—besides which, they're sometimes very useful!

I found the boys from the other papers gathered about the solid-looking door to Spagliotti's suite. As I came into sight there was a chorus of whistles and a few jeers.

"Well, if it isn't little Miss Knowall of the *Record*," said Jack Irby, the Claremont crime man. "Greetings, fair one! But haven't you made some mistake? This is no place for little ladies who report society weddings! This is man's work!"

"Then how is it they ever put you on it?" I asked him, sweetly, and he looked annoyed as the others laughed like a lot of hyenas.

"Gotta hand it to the little lady, there, yes sir, Irby! She sure got the snap in that one!" grinned Mason of the Wire.

"Anything happened yet?" I asked them, and there was a general shaking of heads.

"Flannel's playing it tight again—he won't even let us take a look at the body, let alone make a statement. He's been in there the last hour..."

"Hmm! Have any of you tried to get in?"

"Sure, naturally. But I tell you nobody'll get past that door until Flannel's good and ready—which may be as late as tomorrow lunch time, the speed that guy works at."

I looked round at them, waiting patiently to be admitted. I remembered that it was my job to get something good on this case. I patted my hair, looked at my face in the mirror, straightened my hat and stockings to the accompaniment of appreciative remarks from the boys, then knocked on the room door. It opened, and a large, florid policeman looked out.

"I'm from the *Record*," I told him.

"Are ye, now? And what would ye be wantin' here?"

"I'd like to see the body, please," I said, giving him the biggest helping of charm a man ever got. But I guess he was married with about two dozen kids, for he just grunted, and said:

"So would all the boys out there, but ye'll not be seeing anything at all 'til Inspector Flannel says so! Now be getting back in line, will ye?"

I had to take a chance. I felt sure if I could just get in that room, somehow I'd manage to stay there. I said:

"You don't understand! I have some information for you— concerning the case. Please let the Inspector know I am here."

He looked dubious, but turned round and called: "There be a young lady here, sir, who says she has got some information for ye? Will I be sending her in?"

The irate voice of Flannel drifted back. "What information?"

"She says 'tis regarding the case here. Says she wants to be seeing ye, sir."

There was a sound of steps from within, and the painfully thin, angular features of Detective Inspector Flannel of Homicide peered out at me. I knew him, but I had the advantage, for he had never seen me before. That may sound rather odd, but I knew him from various photos in the paper, from articles about him. He was a clever man, they said, and his perpetual dislike of newspapermen had made him the talk of the press world.

He gave me a keen look, then eyed the other reporters at the back of me.

"When can we have a look at the body, Inspector?" asked Jack Irby, quickly.

"When I'm gone, and you won't annoy me," grunted Flannel. "Until then, keep quiet, or I'll see you're slung out!"

Irby colored up, but he became duly silent. Flannel was about the only man in New York who wasn't afraid of the power of the press—and about the only man who would have had the guts to talk to big-shot reporters that way! He gave me the eye again, said:

"Are you the dame—sorry, I mean lady—who wanted to spill some info on the murder which has taken place here?"

I was somehow afraid now, unaware of just what I would say when he asked me. However, I nodded.

"Okay. Step inside, sister—that is, lady."

I stepped inside to a chorus of enraged howls from the boys. Probably they were all wondering just what I knew about the killing—and so was Flannel. For he was looking at me from cold, keen grey eyes, under shaggy brows.

We were in a kind of anteroom, which connected with all the other rooms in Spagliotti's eight-floor suite. Four doors in all led off it, and behind one of these lay the dead man. But which one? And what good had it done me getting in here? Obviously Flannel hadn't the faintest intention of letting me in to see what was what.

I could have told him something he wanted to know very badly—but I didn't want to! It wouldn't have done—so when he directed those eyes of his at me again, I took a seat on a plush settee which was let into the wall and leaned back, showing him just where the silk tops of my nylons made connection with my suspenders.

He wasn't interested. I could see that.

16

"Have you come here to give a free leg show, lady, or do you really have something to tell me?"

"I do have something to tell you—where have you put the body?"

"Listen, you're supposed to be answering the questions."

"Then suppose you start asking?"

"I will. Just what is it you know?"

"I'd like to see what's left of Spagliotti before I tell you that. And I'd like your opinion of the crime."

Flannel snorted with impatience. He said: "The body's in the kitchen, just where we found it—but you don't get to see it. I'm waiting to hear what you know. Or are you just a news-nose after information?" He had hit the truth that time, and I must have shown it in my face, for he said: "I thought so! Now blow, sister, before I have Murphy here throw you out. I don't like snoopy reporters humming around and getting in everybody's way. Didn't your editor ever tell you the facts of life?"

I decided to try another line. I said: "Give me a break, Inspector. Honest, this means a lot to me. A raise in salary, promotion, and all the rest of it. Be a sport!"

He suddenly grinned and said: "I think you need a lesson— so just for this once I'll give you a break... Maybe after you've seen the state that bird is in you'll think twice about wanting to be a crime reporter!"

He opened a door on the right, and led me in. Spagliotti was lying on the floor, covered by a white sheet. The photographers and finger-printers were just clearing up, having finished with the body. Flannel took my arm and led me forward until we were standing right over Spagliotti.

"Hold on to your hat, sister. Here we go!" His foot hooked into the corner of the shroud, and jerked it away.

I felt my stomach coming up into my throat, and I turned from that fat figure with disgust and horror. You see, Spagliotti hadn't been a good-looking guy in the first place, and the three bullets which had entered the back of his head had taken most of the front of his face with them, destroying any pretensions of looks he had ever had.

It was sticky, messy, and although I had thought it wouldn't shake me, it did. I turned pale, and Flannel led me to a chair and sat me down.

"See?" he queried. "Now maybe you'll go home to your mother!"

CHAPTER 2

I KNOW SOME OF THE ANSWERS

I had a hard—a very hard—struggle to keep from being sick there and then, but eventually, when I had overcome the feeling, and had subdued my nauseated stomach by sheer willpower, I lit a cigarette and inhaled deeply.

Flannel stood watching me, a half-smile on his face. I think he fancied he had given me such a nasty turn I wouldn't ever want to crime report again. That was where he was wrong.

I said: "Well, Mister Flannel, when does something else happen?"

"So, you haven't seen enough, huh? And what do you think is going to happen now?"

"I take it you've found something out—or have you? When, how and why it was done?"

"We found out when—about an hour and a half ago—but we don't know why, and how stumps us, young lady. From enquiries made it seems Spagliotti was up here alone—with the doors of his suite locked. Two of his thugs were standing guard over him in the passage—seems he always has two of the boys to hand—and they swear they heard nothing. That argues that the rod was a silenced one. But they also swear they let no one past them, and when they finally burst down the door, being unable to obtain an answer to their knocking, they found Spagliotti stretched out in the kitchen here."

"What makes you so sure one of his own boys didn't do it?"

"Simply that if they had they'd have got rid of the body without calling in the police. That's elementary, Miss Curzon."

"I understand. Of course, they certainly wouldn't kill him then send for you. Did you find any other clues?"

"We did," he said. He crossed to the table, took a pair of grey leatherette gloves from it, tossed them into my lap. I picked them up and glanced at them. "What have these to do with the case?"

"We don't know—yet! But, they were found near the body, as if they had been dropped in the excitement of the murder..."

"Good Heavens! Surely you don't think a woman..."

"I didn't say so, but that's how it looks. Matter of fact one of Spagliotti's boys says he wouldn't be sure, but he thinks he heard a woman giggling in here just prior to the killing. And as you can see, there're champagne bottles on the table, and two glasses. The boys say they heard the corks of the bottles pop once or twice—-and I expect that's why they didn't hear the pop of the revolver—most likely thought Spagliotti was getting a thirst again."

"Have you tested for fingerprints?"

"Yeah! Nothing doing. What's worrying me is how the dame got past these two thugs and a locked door!"

I let my eyes wander about the room. Then I rose and, carefully avoiding the body, crossed to a smallish, square door in the kitchen wall. "What's this?" I demanded, opening it. I looked down into a deep, dark well.

"Say, I figured that was just a closet," breathed Flannel. "Apparently, it's a service lift. And see here—it can be operated from inside, by anyone pulling on these ropes."

Flannel moved to the door, sent the cop for someone. The cop came back with a thin, weedy, nervous-looking little man, who might have been the manager. He was the manager. Flannel said:

"Where's this service lift lead to?"

The manager wrung his skinny hands and said: "Right down into the kitchens below, Inspector."

"But there's a kitchen here!"

"I know—but in case the tenants wanted meals providing, all they had to do was send their orders through the speaking tube by the side of the lift, and the meal was sent up to them."

"I see. Does this lift connect with any other rooms?"

"No, none at all. We have the lifts arranged so that each suite has its own. Then there's no confusion."

"And how about the kitchens? Who was on duty down there at the time of the murder?"

"No one, Inspector. The chefs and maids all finish at eight o'clock, directly after sending up any dinners ordered. They all live out of the place. The kitchens are left locked and deserted."

"Hmm! So maybe someone could have gotten in with a skeleton key, run themselves up in the lift, and done for Spagliotti!"

"That's all well and good," I said. "But he'd have heard them coming up in the lift! He'd have been ready for trouble."

"That's so, but supposing it was some fancy woman, sneaking in to spend the night with him? Suppose she had a reason for killing him, and he had no idea of her intentions?"

"But why shouldn't she come in the front way?"

"Well, she might have been some society doll, who had a yen for racketeers, but daren't risk the least chance of being associated publicly with one."

I smiled and blew smoke out. "It's a little fantastic, Inspector."

"Maybe it is, and maybe it isn't! I know some of these classy dolls from Park Avenue. Could be she was frightened of him talking—or perhaps the louse was blackmailing her. Anyway, it lines up right to me. The woman came up by the lift and had a drink with Spagliotti. When he turned his back, she let him have it, went out the same way she came, dropping her gloves in her hurry!"

21

"There's just one thing which makes it sound more improbable—those gloves! No society girl would be found dead in them!"

"No? Why what's wrong with them?"

"Nothing's wrong, actually. It's just that they're a cheap line which Macy's stock—one dollar a pair. Alright for a Brooklyn kid to buy his girl, but certainly not fit for a Park Avenue deb."

Flannel looked dumbfounded. He said: "She might have bought them especially for the job!"

"So she might—or she might have left them purposely to put you on a wrong scent."

"Then we'll trace the person who bought them—"

"Don't be an idiot, Inspector. Macy's must sell two or three hundred pairs of those a day. How on earth can you check on casual sales like that?"

Flannel groaned, looked at me again. He said: "You're kind of smart, aren't you?"

"Not at all. Any woman could tell you what I'm telling you!"

He went to the door of the ante-room and barked: "Send in Mugs."

Mugs had been Spagliotti's right-hand man. He was a tall, gorilla-like specimen, with hairy hands and a barrel chest. It wasn't so hard to see how he got the name of Mugs, either. His face had all the appearance of something which had run foul of a steam shovel and had had a couple of tons torn clean from the middle. I had heard of Mugs, but never before had I seen him. And I hoped I never would again. He was a big, stupid, muscle-bound hunk, but I didn't like the way he looked at my crossed legs, so I uncrossed them and pulled down my skirt as far as it would go, over my knees—which wasn't very far, anyway. It was that kind of skirt!

"Now then, Mugs," said Flannel, to the human monkey. "Let's have your full story about what happened. And try to remember just everything you heard behind that door tonight!"

"Uh-huh, 'spector," grinned Mugs, docilely. "Me and Lefty stood guard—Boss said he didn't want no disturbin' tonight, an' warned us there'd be trouble if we did."

"He didn't say anything about entertaining a woman?"

"No, 'spector. We stands guard, an' about nine o'clock we hears corks popping. 'Bout two hours after which, pop goes another. Then we hears a dame—leastways. I think we hears a dame. If it was the boss, he sure went all girlish of a sudden. Anyways, whoever it was, they were gigglin', sort of, and laughin', like as if they had too much giggle water under their snoot. We hears another cork pop, then we don't hear nothin' else. Leastways, not until Lippy comes up wid a message for the boss... Then we knocks, gets no answer. We keeps knockin', and Lippy says something has maybe happened, since we all knows what a weak ticker de boss has. So we do like Lippy says to do and bust the door in. You know what happens next."

"And that's all you know?"

"Sure, that's the lot, 'spector."

"You aren't aware of any woman who might want Spagliotti bumped off?"

"Not a one. Nope!"

"Then maybe you know of some enemies he had?"

Mugs' face brightened, if you could call it a face. He said: "Sure. The boss musta had about a thousand enemies right here in New York. Think of all the things he done, then you can start counting, an' I reckon you'd still be finding people he'd done wrong by this time next century."

"Did he ever do wrong by—you?" snapped Flannel.

"Who me? Sure, he did wrong by all the boys. But that don't say we'd have the nerve to put him on the black dot, 'spector. All of us was sick scared o' the boss. I'm saying so."

Flannel sent him out there, and had Lippy and Lefty called in. Their stories coincided exactly with Mugs'. And that was about all. When Flannel opened the doors and let the news hawks in, I made one big rush for the nearest phone booth, my story all ready

It hit the editions the next day. I'd made the most of it: I put in that I had worked on the spot with Flannel and had given him the means the murderer, or murderess, had used to effect an entry into the suite: the dumb waiter. The story carried my name, and I hinted that I had a fair idea of who had done the killing. I did have—more than a fair idea, really.

I was in a downtown eatery the next day when I spottcd a young, badly-shaven man looking over at me. In spite of the blue shade round his chin he was quite attractive looking—he had a tough kind of face, but the eyes were friendly, and when he smiled the corners of them kind of crinkled up.

He was smiling now, and I patted my back hair into place and moved ever so slightly until he had a good view of my ankles. I was hoping he'd see I wasn't unwilling to eat with him. And he did, for before a minute had elapsed, he came over, with a lazy, yet tense kind of walk. He stood right over me, looking down from slightly lowered eyelids. His glance was mocking but interested.

"Miss Curzon, I presume?" His voice was as mocking as his glance—a kind of lazy drawl that still conveyed an impression of latent power.

I nodded acquiescence. "How did you know my name," I asked.

"Easy! I read your report in the paper, and I've been on your tail since you left the newspaper office an hour ago."

"You—you followed me?"

"Sure, why not? I had a reason, as it happens. But even if I hadn't, I'd still have thought you were well worth following!"

I said: "If you're trying to hand me a line, it won't work. If there's anything you want me for, say so, and we'll see what I can do about it. If not, suppose you leave."

He sat down in the chair near me, leaned towards me, and said: "I'm a private detective—Ross is the name—Edmond Ross. I don't expect you'll have heard of me... We don't move in the same circles. The point is, I've been retained in the Spagliotti murder—"

I admit this made me sit up and take notice. I said: "By whom?"

"No reason you shouldn't know. By Mugs and the rest of the boys. They want to know who did it, but quick. Then I expect they'll take their own revenge—and it won't be a pleasant one."

I shuddered. I had a fair idea what the gang would do to the killer of their leader, if the killer could be found. "And...?"

"From your column in the *Record* this morning, you seem to know quite a bit about how it was done, and you said you had an idea of who did it. Is that right?"

I admitted it was.

"Then perhaps you'll give me a lead on it?"

"Sorry."

"You won't?"

"You'd better get me straight, Mister Ross. I have an idea—but I've no intention of helping to bring to justice the killer of Spagliotti! He deserved death—and I think whoever did it ought to get a medal. But they won't... If the gang gets them, they'll get tortured—killed. If the State get them they'll go to the pen for a long time. So, you see, I prefer to keep it to myself."

"You're sure you won't spill?"

"Positively."

He looked regretful. He glanced towards the other end of the room, and I saw none other than Mugs approaching. He said: "You asked for this, baby!"

Mugs came right up to the table, one hand in his pocket. I could make out the shape of an automatic in that hand, under the cloth. He said: "Get up! You're goin' wid us, lady!"

CHAPTER 3

NO PLACE FOR A LADY!

I got up. I went with them. What else could I do? I knew Mugs' reputation well enough to know that even if he wouldn't have used the gun there and then, he'd have let me have it later on I had refused to obey him.

They took me to a parked car away along the street, and indicated that I should hop in, which I did. There was no effort at concealment; they simply drove me through Lower Manhattan and down near the Hudson. Here we stopped, and alighted. They took me into a shop which had once been a Chinese laundry belonging to a gentleman by the name Ah Wong Ho but was now deserted. There was a trap door in the floor, and they hauled this up and shoved me down on to the wooden steps. I went down, perilously, for the steps were rickety and narrow.

There were a number of candles lit in that cellar, and seated around on upturned rotted old washtubs, were Lefty and Lippy, whom I've mentioned, I think, before. I hadn't ever seen them until the night of Spagliotti's killing, but there wasn't much mistaking which was which. Lippy was thin and emaciated, dapperly dressed, with a flamboyant tie. The lip from which he derived his nickname jutted out under his nose, and almost covered the cigarette he was smoking.

Lefty, on the other hand, was six foot two of raw-boned Bronx tough—a figure the size and shape of a prize pig, and a face which would have discredited a gorilla in the Bronx Zoo. He sat chewing gum, spitting from time to time at a small beetle which was crawling leisurely across the stone-flagged floor.

When we arrived, the two of them stood up, and Lefty ground a large boot on that beetle with an air of finality.

"So you gots her, eh?" said Lippy, his protuberant lip twisting upwards into what might be called a smile.

"Yeah—I went out to get her, didn't I?" said Mugs.

"Sure, sure. An' she wouldn't spill nothings to Ross?"

"Not a thing," said Edmond Ross.

I looked at him with contempt in my gaze and thought that he wasn't half so good looking as I had thought at first.

"Siddown!" grunted Mugs.

I made like he said. I 'saddown.'

"Now look here," Ross began, "you can save yourself a lot of trouble if you simply tell us all you know about Spagliotti's murder."

"I don't know anything, I tell you."

"Is that so? Not long ago you told me you knew plenty!"

"Oh, I was just talking, that's all. I wanted to make myself seem…important."

"Is that so? An' how about what you said in the paper? Didn't you say you had a damned good idea of who done it?"

"Do you believe everything you read in papers, Mister Ross?"

"Not everything—just what I want to."

"I put that in, about knowing more than I cared to say about the murder, just to give myself a lift. You know, it made good copy."

"Is that so?"

I grimaced. "Mister Ross, if you don't stop saying 'Is that so' shortly, you will drive me crazy!"

"Is that—that is, look here, Miss Curzon. We don't want to have to hurt you—but we can do so, remember. If you know anything at all about this affair, why not make a clean breast of it?"

I shook my head: "You're wasting your time, Mister Ross!"

Mugs stepped forward, and he didn't look so cool any more. He growled: "I told you youse wouldn't get no place usin' that soft line, Ross. You gotta be tough ... lemme try!"

Ross stepped back, and Mugs stepped forward. He brandished a ham-sized fist in front of my nose. He said: "See that?"

"I'd have to be blind not to," I remarked "What size gloves do you take?"

"Yeah? Okay, smart dame! You'll smart more when we're through. Now, either spill what you know, or else."

I knew I was in an awful spot. I wasn't playing with kids; these thugs could really work on me, and if they did so, I knew that, after a few moments of their methods, I'd tell them all I knew about Spagliotti and who killed him. And that would never have done!

"Listen," I pleaded, desperately. "What's worrying you? Now your boss has gone, you can pull the same jobs, and you needn't give him the lion's share of the proceeds. So why worry?"

"I tell you why, sister. Because I don't like the way the boss was bumped off, that's why. There's a difference between a gang killing and the way the boss was fixed. If it had been Jake Stewman or any of his boys, they wouldn't have committed the murder the way this was committed. Which argues that it is someone who happens to have a personal kick against Spagliotti. An' if they bumped the boss, who's to say they won't get ambitious and start disliking me, or Lefty, or Lippy next? Who's to say they ain't planning to send us on a one-way journey?"

There was nothing wrong with his logic there. But I said: "What's making you so darned sure it wasn't some other racketeer who killed him?"

"I told you, it isn't a gang killing. Us guys don't go about the job the way an amateur would—we just let 'em have it, and

29

rely on alibis, and lack of clues, to throw the cops on the wrong scent. But this was done stealthy, get me?"

"I see."

"Now come on, talk! Maybe you think it was Iris Van Woden?"

"Who? Good heavens, no! Why should I think it was she?"

"Well, I don' mind tellin' ya: the Van Woden floozie had a yen for the boss—an' he was soakin' her good an' plenty for blackmail... Maybe she was kiddin' along she was stuck on him, an' meant to bump him all the time!"

I laughed. Actually, Iris Van Woden was the last person I would have thought of in connection with murder. I had interviewed her for the paper, on what the deb is wearing this season, and had found her a regular character. She was pretty, with a smug, superior prettiness which all these debs seem to cultivate. But brother, was she brainless! She dithered and dathered, and in the end I had to write the whole interview from my own head, for nothing she told me was of the slightest use.

She didn't seem to think it was a fashion interview; she seemed rather to imagine the reason for my visit was to find out how many boyfriends she had had, and who they were. Anyway, that was all I could get out of her. I gathered the impression that, so far, two counts, three dukes, one prime minister and a local ice-man had all committed suicide because of her fatal beauty. Which was, to say the least, unlikely.

And it was this specimen who Mugs suspected!

"No," I told him. "I'm quite certain it wasn't Iris V.W. She wouldn't have the brains to plan a crime like that!"

"Then who is it you do figure done it, lady?"

"I told you. I haven't the faintest idea!"

Mugs' face went black with anger. He raised his big fist and struck me across the mouth, knocking me spinning from the barrel top I had sat down on. I felt one of my teeth crunch and the salt blood ran over my tongue, which I had bitten half through.

I lay there, a little dazed, and when I was able to take a further interest in the proceedings, I noticed an argument had started up.

Edmond Ross, the tough detective, was standing facing Mugs, his hands balled into fists, his eyes flashing annoyance. Mugs was wearing a surprised look, as if he had been bitten by a dog he was feeding. Ross was saying: "I understood you said we'd bring her down here to try and scare the truth out of her?"

"Did I? Well, maybe she don't scare easy! So what? We got to try other methods now, ain't we?"

"No! Personally, I don't think the kid knows a thing. Like she told you, it was all a big act, calculated to higher her prestige."

"You think so, huh?"

"I'm sure."

Mugs' eyes narrowed to tiny, fleshy slits in his lumpy face. His voice ground out: "If you don't like our methods, then blow, will ya! I hired you to trace the boss's murderer, see, not to tell me what, an' what not, to do. So far you ain't been any help whatsoever. You reckoned you could pump this Jane without having to get tough—you had your chance, an' you balled it up. So now we do it our way! You don't like it done that way—beat it! An' hand back that century I paid you for a retainer!"

Ross clenched his hands, but he stepped back and stood silent. Mugs sneered over at him, and pulled me up from the floor. He hauled me towards him, pulling on my wrists, until my back was hard against his chest and stomach. My arms were twisted up towards the back of my head and were giving me agony. He said: "No use to scream, lady. Nobody c'n hear you from here. Now will you talk some?"

"I swear I don't—know—anything," I almost sobbed.

31

Mugs said: "Lippy—show the pretty lady your little knife, huh? Show her your shiv, pal. Lippy does some very nice carvings in wood with his little knife, lady, and I happen to know that once or twice he's done some in human flesh, also! Show her, Lippy!"

"It's a pleasure, Mugs," leered Lippy. He came over and stood about two feet in front of me. He twitched a razor-sharp knife from his sheath on the forearm. He made a few passes.

"Think what damage that could do to a pretty dame like you!" gloated Mugs. "An' remember, we ain't kiddin'. Now talk!"

"But I honestly don't know anything," I cried. "I—I'd tell you if I could…."

Mugs said, with a snarl: "Okay, Lippy, give it to her!"

Lippy said: "The pleasure's all mine." He stepped up to within a few inches of me, twisted his dirty fingers in the neckline of my blouse, and wrenched. Even Lefty spat out his gum and came over to survey me with interest.

Lippy's fingers clawed up to the top of my slip—I shrank away, shuddering from his lewd hands. Then he had ripped the slip, too, and I stood in front of them, burning with shame.

Lippy raised his knife, whet it with his thumb, brought it into line with my breasts....

"Hold it! Don't make another move!" grated Ross from the back of the cellar. They all spun towards him, open-mouthed. Ross gazed at them grimly, over the barrel of an automatic. He said: "I told you I thought the kid didn't know anything. And I still think so. But in any event, I guess I don't care to stand for dames being manhandled. So let go of her arms, Mugs, or maybe this rod'll go off!"

"Yeah?" sneered Mugs, "and the slug'd hit the lady!" That was right; I was directly in the line of fire, unable to move a muscle.

32

Ross's eyes had shifted momentarily to Mugs, and Lippy, who still held his shiv, saw his opportunity and took it. His hand went back, forwards, and a shimmering streak darted for the detective's face. Ross ducked, dodged it, but it gave the two racketeers their chance. Before he could level the gun again, they were on him, reaching for their own revolvers.

Lippy didn't last a second. Ross's gun smashed down on his skull the minute he was near enough, and Lippy folded up like an old concertina and hit the stone floor with his nose. Lefty got his head down and butted. Ross staggered back, his wind driven from his body in a great gasp. While he was still doubled up, Lefty tried to kick his face. Ross hadn't been so bad as he had made out, for as Lefty's foot rose and sailed at his mouth he grabbed it, twisted it, half turned and threw, and Lefty floated through the air gracefully, only managing to stop by letting his big chin smack against the wall. After which he joined Lippy on the floor.

Meanwhile, Mugs had been groping for his revolver, and had found it. As Lefty threw in the towel, he brought it up, hanging onto me with one hand, and took aim at Ross.

There was only one thing I could think of to save the young shamus from those hot slugs, and I did it: I threw myself back with all my force against Mugs. The gun exploded, and the slug whistled harmlessly into the air and cut into the wooden crossbeams under the ceiling.

Then Ross was over; I felt his fist sizzle past my ear with tremendous force, and I heard it detonate against Mugs' jaw. The grip on my arms was released, and Mugs slumped slowly in the same direction as his cronies.

"I'm afraid," said Ross, regretfully, "that I've broken the poor fellow's jaw! However, I expect it'll get well again in no time, and if he values his well-being, he really shouldn't stick it out so much!"

Ross had saved me from something which could have been very nasty. I was still in a state of shock. All I could gasp was, "Thanks!"

"A mere trifle!" he smiled. "And now, suppose we beat it out of here? The dump gives me the heebie-jeebies! Let's go find the nearest bar, where we can grab a drink or so—I need one after the kick in the guts I took from our sprawled-out friend down there!"

I followed him up the cellar steps...but not until he had relieved his victims of their wallets!

CHAPTER 4

INSPECTOR FLANNEL GETS IDEAS

We settled down in a nearby saloon, and Edmond—as I was now calling him—ordered whisky, straight. It isn't really my drink, but I thought I needed it after what had just happened, and, sure enough, it did me good.

We drank, ordered again, and relaxed. Then Edmond said: "That was a hot spot you were in—I'm sorry I had a hand leading you into it."

"Why did you help them?"

"Listen," he said, leaning forward. "I'm a private dick. I find it hard to live these days. I'm glad to grab any job I can, and Mugs offered me big dough. I couldn't afford to turn it down—big dough, I mean. When they said they intended to grab you off and question you, I persuaded them to let me try it the easy way first. That didn't work, so I had to play along and help snatch you—but I honestly didn't have any idea they'd get tough with you. The idea was to scare you out of your pants, get you to squawk—you believe me, don't you? I'm levellin' with you."

"I believe you, of course. If it hadn't been so, you'd not have gone to so much trouble to help me, would you?"

"I surely wouldn't."

"And now you've lost the money they'd have paid you for your services. Too bad, Edmond."

"Not so bad, really."

He flicked out the three wallets he had lifted from the three crooks, and revealed the interiors, brimming with notes.

"That's another thing—" I said. "I hadn't expected you to—steal from them."

"No? An' why not? They'll do no squawking about this little lot—they daren't! Why shouldn't I lift the mazuma of guys like those?"

I shrugged. "They may not squawk to the police, but if I know anything about Mugs, he'll he out to get you after what you did. He won't rest until he's qualified you for six feet of loose earth!"

"He isn't the only mug who's wanted to do that," laughed Edmond. "And I guess he won't be the last, either. Maybe it's he who'll get the earth. I'm no schoolboy, myself, Anita!"

"I can see that. But…well, look out for yourself. What do you intend to do about all this? Drop the whole matter?"

He knitted his brows and frowned deeply. He said: "No. No, I'm not dropping it. I'm kind of interested myself—you know how it is with these mysteries. No, I'm going right on with the investigation." He went on, when I did not reply: "Do you really know who it was?"

"I'd prefer not to talk about that, if you don't mind."

"But you know definitely it wasn't the Van Woden dame?"

"Definitely. That's as much as I'll say!"

"Hmm! There must be hundreds—thousands—of people who bore Spagliotti some kind of grudge. One of them did this job—but how could anyone sort the right one out from the mob which Spagliotti wronged? It'd be impossible!"

"Forget it," I said. "If you're nice I'll allow you to take me to see the Yehudi Menuhin concert at Carnegie tonight…"

"Forget that—you'd never get tickets. The joint'll be sold out."

"Don't forget, I'm with the press. I've got passes."

"You have?"

"I have! Any amount, for everything from the Menuhin concert to Earl Carroll's Vanities."

He stood up, said: "I'll blow now, I expect you have to go back to the news office. I'll pick you up at seven tonight; don't forget to bring the passes!"

"I won't," I promised. "I'm looking forward to seeing the concert."

"To hell with the concert—I mean the passes for the Vanities!"

Then he was gone, leaving me with a smile on my face.

* * * *

But as it happened, we never got as far as the Vanities. He called for me promptly at seven, as promised, but as we were preparing to leave, the phone rang. It was Claxon again. He said: "Listen, Anita. You've been handling the Spagliotti killing so far, and I think you want to go on handling it?"

"Naturally."

"Okay. A lead just came in—if you're busy I'll give it to one of the boys—but that stuff you did for today's edition is great, and I'd like you to follow it up. What'd you say?"

"I'll follow it up—what's the assignment?"

"Down at Headquarters—Flannel just arrested Iris Van Woden for the murder of Spagliotti! Get down there and see what you can get hold of."

"On my way," I told him. I hooked the receiver and turned to Edmond. "I won't be able to make it for the show," I told him. "So, suppose you go, and I'll meet you afterwards?"

"Why? What's broken?"

"Only our date."

"Come on, give. Is it something on the killing?"

I sighed. I said: "Yes, that's it."

"Mind if I come along?"

"I don't—but I'm afraid you won't get in unless you're a reporter."

"Then I'll be a reporter—you got a spare pass?"

"Yes, I do have a spare press card here, but…"

"But nothing! Flannel's an old friend of mine. The guy loves me. It'll be okay, once I'm in. Let's go!"

There was no arguing with him at all. He stowed my old press card in his pocket, and we left the apartments. We took a cab at the corner and were driven swiftly to Headquarters.

The passes got us right inside all right. There were the other boys, and there was Detective Inspector Flannel trying to shout them down.

"So, you found the blackmail letters—the letters which Van Woden wrote to Spagliotti—and you also learned he was bleeding her plenty…"

"You say she didn't have an alibi? Spent the night walking around?"

"Take it easy, you bloodhounds," bawled Flannel. "Cool off, and when I'm good and ready you'll get a statement."

"What makes you so certain it was Van Woden, Inspector?"

"I'll tell you if you'll pipe down a bit. It was the night porter—he said he spotted Iris Van Woden sneaking down the area leading to the kitchen entrance of Spagliotti's hotel."

"Great! But that doesn't prove she killed him!"

"No, it doesn't. But the porter's definite—and so is the cab driver who drove her there—that was about an hour before the murder happened! And we also found the guy who drove her home again—fifteen minutes after Spagliotti had been murdered! He said she seemed to be in an agitated state, and also that there was blood on her coat sleeve! We found the coat in her closet at home, and we had the blood analysed. It was Spagliotti's type, okay. And there were four or five hairs from his head on her coat, too. How about that?"

"You seem to have cinched it, Inspector. How about letting us have a statement from the dame? Let's see her, huh?"

Flannel said: "Okay. But make it snappy."

He led us through to where the detention cells were, Iris Van Woden was in the end one, and they had made her as comfortable as possible.

She was reclining on the bench which the police had strewn with all the cushions they could get hold of, and she was reading a cheap novel. Every line of her, every gesture, was an act. She was still acting, here, in jail, with the shadow of Sing Sing hanging over her. She looked up as we gathered outside her cell, and said, brightly: "Awf'ly nice of you boys to come!"

She simpered at us, swung her legs off the bench, so that the folds of her exclusive, hundred-dollar skirt pulled up over her knees. She had nice knees like the rest of her. She was all nice, Iris Van Woden. Her hair was gold, done in an elaborate page-boy style; her teeth were pure white, and matched well with her dimpled cheeks. Her lips were full and red and sensuous. She looked quite sweet, and innocent. Her wide, baby blue eyes stared at us, smilingly, and she moved again so that every curve of her figure was outlined against, the dark black of her blouse.

"How about a statement, Miss Van Woden?"

"Statement? Well, all I can say is that I didn't do it—! I mean it's so silly, isn't it? Someone will get into most awful trouble about this. I mean my father won't stand for it, you know. It's so—so—what is the word I want? So degrading,"

"You still say you didn't kill him?"

"My dear men, of course not! What makes you think I could do such a thing?"

"You're pretty fond of talking about all the guys who killed themselves for love of you—maybe this one wouldn't get in line like the others, and you had to kill him yourself!"

"How dare you! I never saw the fellow in my life!"

"You deny having visited him that night?"

"Emphatically!"

"In spite of three witnesses?"

39

"Yes!"

It was obvious that Iris couldn't bring herself really to believe she was in serious danger of having the murder pinned on to her. And I knew she hadn't done it—it amazed me anyone could think, for one minute, that she had.

She went on, dimpling prettily: "You boys will be kind to me in your reports, won't you? I mean you won't publish any of those horrible photographs of me. At least, not unless they do me credit. And none of those disgusting headlines like: 'Love Nest Slaying,' and that sort of thing. Suppose you just put 'Innocent Girl Arrested for Death of Man She has Never Even Seen!'"

"That'd be rather a long headline," grinned one of the boys.

"Oh, well, something like that, you know."

"I'm afraid that's out of our hands—a special staff man does the headlines, and bills."

Flannel stepped forward and growled. "C'mon now. Beat it and give the lady a bit of peace. You got your stories, haven't you? G'wan then!" He ushered the boys out, and as he did so, Edmond slipped over to the cell and said:

"Miss Van Woden, I'm a private detective. If I can help you in any way…"

"That's very, very sweet of you. Yes, I do believe you can help me—if you can find the horrible person who murdered that terrible man, I'd be so glad. My father would pay you well, Mister...?"

"Ross. Edmond Ross. Very well, Miss Van Woden—I'll take it that you have retained me."

"Do, please. Probably my father will also engage investigators, but the more the merrier. Of course, it's all so ridiculous, you know. I wouldn't harm a teeny mouse, let alone a great big bad gangster."

Ross couldn't help grinning. He turned back to me.

"Well, now you have another job," I told him.

40

"Yes, I have. Suppose you save me a lot of trouble and spill all you know?"

"Sorry—I'm a clam again. I know nothing."

"You're an enigmatical little devil, aren't you?" he grinned.

There was a sudden roar of wrath from the doorway. It was Flannel! "What the hell are you two doing here? And... Holy Mike! Ross! Edmond Ross! How did you get in? I'll fire the man who let a bum dick into this place! Who was it, you skunk?"

"See," Edmond said, turning to me with a grin. "I told you the Inspector knew and loved me! See how glad he is to see me?"

"Who let you in?" rumbled Flannel.

"I sneaked in, Inspector. No one's to blame."

"Sneaked in, did you? Har! Well sneak out again, quick!"

"Take it easy, Inspector. I've been here to interview one of my clients, see?"

"What?"

"That's right—Miss Van Woden! I'm making it my job to find the man, or the woman, who really murdered Spagliotti—and then will your face be red!"

"Pah! If you have as much luck on this as you had of your other cases, Iris Van Woden's as good as in the pen right now!" Edmond just grinned exasperatingly, and Flannel roared: "And in future, if you want to know something from the lady, do it through her lawyers! I won't have trash like you littering the station up! Now blow and take this smart lady reporter with you! From her article on the yellow rag she works for, you'd think she discovered the murder, and took charge of the whole investigation. I'm given credit for nothing! 'Reporter Gives Police Inspector Important Information!' Bah!"

We went, hurriedly. If we hadn't, I'm afraid Flannel would just have burst into enraged pieces there and then....

41

CHAPTER 5

NAME THE KILLER, LADY!

Edmond was strangely silent on the way back to my apartment. I didn't know what was eating him, but somehow the whole night had been ruined. He wasn't the same—he seemed to draw himself into himself, and hardly spoke to me at all.

It was reasonably early when we got back, and I said: "Like to come up for a drink, Edmond?"

He shook his head. "I guess not, I figure I'll be pushing along…."

"Oh," I said, rather flatly, and I won't deny I was disappointed. "Then—when'll I see you again?"

"Oh, I dunno. Around. I guess. Maybe I'll call you up…"

"Maybe?"

"Yeah, that's what I said—just maybe!"

He didn't say anything else—just turned and walked off down the street, leaving me standing there, gazing blankly after him. I was hurt, more so because that blue stubble chin of his had by now got a fatal fascination for me, and I had reckoned he felt the same way about me—but seemingly not. Something was wrong, but I'm no mind reader, and he hadn't given me any indication of what the trouble was.

I shrugged my shoulders and went along to my rooms. I phoned my story in to Claxon, and he was tickled silly with the whole affair.

"Great," he said. "Swell story."

"Listen, Claxon," I told him. "Make sure you print it like I gave it to you—at least in the essential facts. Make it plain that we don't believe the Van Woden bird really did do it!"

"But we can't, Anita. You know very well this paper never takes definite sides. Why buck against the cops?"

"Why? Simply because I happen to know that Iris Van Woden did not do it, that's why!"

"Then who did?"

"Maybe Father Christmas did."

"Huh, smart talk, hey? Listen, unless you can name the actual killer, how can you be certain who did or didn't do it?"

"I can name the actual killer!"

"What?"

"But I don't intend to," I said, sweetly, and replaced the receiver on the hooks.

It was only nine o'clock and I felt dead tired, for it had been a very stirring day. I yawned, slipped off my clothes and piled into bed. I couldn't get to sleep right away, and I tossed and turned, the case running round and round in my head 'til I felt dizzy. I remember hearing a clock strike twelve before I finally dozed off.

I was awakened by a persistent buzzing at my doorbell and murmuring a mild 'damn' under my breath, I climbed into my gown and mules and went to the door.

Edmond was standing outside, looking very thoughtful and serious. I must have stared at him in surprise, for he said: "Don't get alarmed—everything's okay. Aren't you going to invite, me inside?"

"What time is it?"

"About one thirty—what's that to do with it?"

"Oh. Nothing—only it isn't customary for ladies to have strange men in their rooms after midnight—or even before for that matter!"

"Mid-Victorian stuff," he said, and entered without any further argument. He sat down on the edge of my bed and lit a cigarette. I waited somewhat impatiently, for after the rude way he had left me earlier I thought he had a fine nerve coming back this way, as if I was his mistress. Obviously, he didn't care

43

about my reputation—didn't even care whether I had one or not!

Finally, I broke the ice. I said: "That was a fine way to go off earlier! What was wrong with you? Remember a previous date? Or don't I use perfume?"

"That's what I came back for," he said.

"What? To tell me I should use perfume?"

"No—don't clown. You know darned well you smell as sweet as a lily. No, I came back here to tell you why I left you so abruptly earlier." He fell silent again.

"Well, go on! Or have you changed your mind again?"

"No, I haven't. I may as well spit it out. It's this way: Fact is, I'm by way of being very surprised at you, Anita! You admit freely you know who the murderer is—yet you also insist it isn't Iris V. Woden. In that case, hadn't you better come out with the truth?"

"I told you why I didn't want to reveal the killer's name!"

"Yeah, I know. Because you thought he did a public service in bumping off Spagliotti. That's fine and dandy, and I'd agree with you instantly if no one else stood in danger of getting stuck with the rap. But this society dame does, and I now think it's high time you stepped up and spoke your piece and cleared her!"

"Oh, you don't understand. If she was in real danger of being convicted, I'd step up quick enough. But she isn't. Not yet. I want to wait a while, first."

"You may wait too long! Does the killer know that you know he did it?"

"What makes you think it's a he?"

"Isn't it?"

"Sorry—I prefer to keep that to myself! Yes, the killer knows I know..."

"Then suppose he kills you…"

"The killer wouldn't do that. I can assure you, Edmond."

44

"Hmm! I wouldn't be too certain about that. But just in case he does Woden'd be in a fine mess then, wouldn't she?"

I shook my head. "I told you there isn't any possibility of the killer going after me. Please believe that, Edmond."

He wasn't satisfied. He began to argue with me, trying to convince me it would be the right thing to tell all I knew. And finally, being awfully worried myself, and not liking to let Iris Van Woden face the music for someone else, I promised that I would go round to Headquarters the following night and tell all.

Edmond's face cleared, and he said: "Atta girl! I knew you had the stuff in you—an' I'll be right alongside of you when you go! I'm pretty anxious to find out the identity of this mysterious killer myself!"

We had a drink together, and then I saw him to the door. He put his hands on my shoulders, looked into my eyes, and said: "I like you a lot, and I didn't want to think you were shielding a killer from the cops at the cost of an innocent girl."

I smiled, a little wistfully. It was nice to hear him say things like that, but it wasn't much use—not now. "I wonder if you'll feel quite so happy after I've told them what I know?" I queried.

"After? I'll feel happier! I'll know I wasn't wrong in thinking you're a swell baby! Just you get down there tomorrow and name the killer, and then we'll pick things up from there between us..." And he leaned forward, slowly, and pressed his lips against mine....

After that, for the moment, I forgot all about the killer, and I was even glad I'd promised to let out my carefully guarded secret—at the moment.

But in the cold, harsh light of morning, realities were so much nearer, and I was sorry I had been so hasty. Iris Van Woden wasn't even due for trial for ages: I could safely have kept things to myself for some time, and by then something might have happened to throw the guilt off her.

However, I'd promised, and a promise is sacred, at least with me. I had to grin a bit to myself at the idea of the killer trying to kill me because I knew too much! Edmond, poor dear, didn't know just how impossible that was. But he would tonight—and then he'd be real cut up about the whole thing. Or so I hoped!

But not half so cut up as I would be!

I got out of bed and took my shower. I dressed in my sheerest undies—I thought that after I'd told the police what I had to tell with regard to the killer, I probably wouldn't be able to wear anything like sheer silk for some time to come.

I was preoccupied all day, and barely managed to amble through my duties. At seven o'clock, Edmond called for me, to take me along to the police depot. He grinned at me and said: "Say, you look real swell. Not changed your mind, have you?"

I shook my head and smiled: "No, I promised. But I must say I'm sorry that I did promise, now. You rushed me!"

"Forget it, honey. You'll feel better when you've got it off your chest!"

"Perhaps. Well, shall we go?"

We found Flannel at Headquarters, and he showed us into his own private office. He said: "So you've something important to say, eh? Well, it'd better be good. Last time you cracked that line you were just noseying! So it wouldn't be advisable to try it twice!"

"It's all right, Mister Flannel. I do have something important to tell you—the name of the real killer!"

"Are you on the level?" His keen grey eyes pierced clean through me and looked puzzled.

"I'm sorry to say I am!"

"Then go ahead—I'll get Sergeant Ellis here to take down your statement."

"Not so fast, Inspector. First of all, there's one little thing I want you to get right...can you bring Miss Van Woden in here?"

He scratched his grey head and frowned. "I guess so—but are you sure this is a straight deal? You ain't just playing for more newspaper stories, are you?"

"I swear I'm on the level, Inspector."

He nodded and motioned to a patrolman by the door. The patrolman went out, and came back soon with Iris Van Woden.

She wasn't looking as certain of herself as she had the night previous. Her eyes looked red and inflamed and I think she'd been crying more than a little. Her fingers plucked nervously at the hem of her expensive skirt, and she sat on the edge of her chair in a manner that indicated her nerves were torn to shreds. Surprising what one night in jail will do to someone who isn't used to it!

When she spoke, all the Park Avenue had gone from her voice, and it might have been plain Mary Doaks talking. I looked her straight in the eyes and smiled reassuringly at her. "Don't worry," I said. "I'm here to get you out of this scrape. But you must tell the truth; then I can show the Inspector how it happened that, although you were on the scene of the crime, you didn't actually do it. You were up in Spagliotti's place when the murder took place, weren't you?"

She glanced around huntedly but saw nothing except kindly faces. She hesitated a second, no more. Her spirit was broken. She said, in a scarcely audible whisper: "Yes—I—I was!"

"But you—didn't see the murder take place?"

"Nun—no! I didn't see who killed Spagliotti."

"Suppose you make a clean breast of it all? Everything you say will be treated as a confidence, be sure of that. Then, when we know just what happened to you, I'll put the finishing touches to the story, and explain who killed the man and why."

47

She dabbed her eyes with a wisp of lace and nodded. "All right—I—I will. But please—please don't let the newspapers get hold of—of the story, will you?"

"I promise you they won't. Don't be afraid. Just tell us all that took place between yourself and Spagliotti."

"Well, I'd known him for some time, ever since I met him at a party one of my friends gave. I always did admire racketeers, and he was the first I had ever met. I started visiting him at his apartment and staying the—the night." She gulped and went on: "I'm afraid I wrote him some letters, and they were so—so—romantic—I wouldn't have liked the Press to have seen them. After a time, he threatened to send them to the newspapers, and copies of each to my friends and family, if I didn't pay him so much money each time I visited him."

"And you still went to see him after that?"

"I had to—if I hadn't gone he'd have sent those letters out as he said. But I made plans for getting them back. I had a talk with one of his gang—a foreigner called Lippy. Lippy said he'd get the letters back from Spagliotti's safe for me if I paid him five thousand dollars. I paid him half, and said he'd get the rest when I got the letters.

"That particular night I sneaked up to the apartment in the usual manner, by the lift. I knew Lippy was coming along later, and it was my job to drug Spagliotti's drink so that he would be asleep when Lippy arrived to break into the safe. But he must have suspected something—perhaps I showed it. Whatever it was he kept his eyes on me all the time, and I didn't have the least chance to carry out my part of the plan. Then soon we both heard the lift coming up....

"Spagliotti knew I didn't want to be seen there, so he pushed me in a corner cupboard, and locked the door on me. I stayed, there, hardly breathing, wondering what Lippy would do when he saw Spagliotti wasn't unconscious as planned. And it wasn't two minutes after that that I heard the shots!

"They sounded muffled, as if they came from the kitchen. There were three shots, then I heard a body falling to the floor. There was more silence for about ten minutes, and I stayed there in a silent panic, too afraid to call out. I didn't know if Lippy had killed Spagliotti, or vice versa.

"Everything was silent after that—for perhaps another five minutes. Then I heard someone moving about, and soon after I heard Lippy gently calling my name. I answered him, and he let me out of the cupboard.

"He looked pale and agitated, and when I stepped out, he said: 'The boss is done for. We'll have to scram out of here right aways.' I asked him if he had got the letters, and he shook his head. 'No, I didn't get the letters—he's changed the combinations of his safes.'

"Then he took me through the kitchen to the lift, and I saw Spagliotti! He was a horrible sight, lying on his face, and I knelt down by him to see if he were really dead. He was, and I suppose that's where I got the blood on my coat from. I said to Lippy: 'Oh, how awful. You shouldn't have done this!' And he stared at me and said: 'Me? What you talking about? I never done this. I thought you did?'

"'How could I?' I demanded. 'When I was locked up in there! I just heard the shots—muffled, as if they came from a silenced gun!' 'Holy Geez!' he said. 'Then it musta been that dame which I sees sneaking down the area when I am comings up! She musta been up here!'

"I didn't have time to ask him anymore, for he just shoved me into a passing taxicab, and that was the last I saw of him." She stopped talking, and it was clear she had told her story, and one I believed to be true.

"Now," said Flannel, "it seems we have a much clearer idea of what's what. You don't need to name the killer after all, Miss Curzon. Seemingly Lippy did it...."

"But..." I began, blankly.

I had only got that one solitary word out when things began to happen, fast. The window behind Flannel's desk was crashed through, and we more or less all saw the snub nose of a Thompson jutting through the broken glass. And we also saw the ugly face of Mugs behind it. Then Edmond had flung himself sideways, carrying me with him, and Flannel was hugging the floor and shouting: "Duck!"

His voice was drowned out by the harsh chattering tone of the sub-machine gun...

CHAPTER 6

EXIT IRIS VAN WODEN

From where Edmond had pushed me, I could see the whole of the room, now a nest of flying bullets. I could see them spraying up the wall opposite the window, and I could see Iris Van Woden, right in the line of fire, looking sillier than she ever looked before, collapsing and holding her stomach where a patch of messy redness was showing.

Then, abruptly the bullets ceased, the window glass shattered some more as the gun was withdrawn, and the noise of a car motor was audible roaring away.

It had all happened in a matter of seconds.

We came to our feet, and stood looking at each other, blankly. Flannel was behind the desk, still, a stream of blue ink running down his face from an overturned well; Edmond and I were safe against the right-hand wall; the Sergeant was kneeling, holding a shattered wrist; and Iris Van Woden...

Iris was dead all right—she'd never be deader!

She was finished. The bullets had almost sawn her in half. She was lying in front of the desk, crumpled up foolishly, a mildly surprised expression on her face. It had been quick.

Then Flannel was bellowing instructions to the excited men who had thronged into the doorway, and a number of them left at a run to trail the escape car.

Flannel said: "Did anyone see who was at back of that gun?"

"Mugs was," I told him. "Mugs threatened to kill the one who'd murdered Spagliotti—he kept his word, all right."

"But," pointed out Edmond, "he apparently killed the wrong one! Seemingly it was Lippy he should have gunned for!"

"That's so. But how the devil did he know we were in here?"

"Might have been hanging round—watching for a chance to bump off Van Woden—probably read in the papers that she was held for the killing. Perhaps he heard us talking—your window is slightly open at the top, Inspector."

"Then it's too bad he didn't hear about Lippy!"

"Well," rumbled Flannel, morosely. "We may have a fresh lead on the murderer, but we've also got a fresh murder!"

"Which won't be so hard to pin on to the right guy," pointed out Edmond, "because you have three witnesses who spotted Mugs operating that gun."

"There is that—but we've got a fresh corpse! What was it you were going to tell us, Miss Curzon?" said Flannel, sighing wearily.

I stammered: "Oh, I—I—"

Edmond shot a keen glance at me.

"Well, you—you what?" snapped Flannel.

I ran a trembling hand over my temples and said:

"If you don't mind, Mister Flannel, I'll tell you some other time—it—it wasn't really very important!"

"I thought you said you were going to name the killer?"

"Oh—it—it was only a suspicion. Now that Iris has named Lippy, I think my guess must be wrong. I don't wish to throw any suspicion on an innocent person!"

Flannel looked deep into my eyes for a long minute. Then he shrugged and said: "Okay. If you get around to the point where you feel like talking, drop in on me!"

"I will, I promise! Edmond, will you take me home? I—I don't feel too good."

I didn't, either. I felt as sick as—well, as hell! My whole insides were struggling to come up through my throat, and I had a hard fight to keep them down. I'm not tough, never have been, and already I was beginning to detest this crime

52

reporting, and to wish I was back covering dog shows and baby shows at Madison Square.

But I wasn't. I was in this up to the neck, and there was no way out for me now, until the episode was closed. I wondered just how it would close? Would they—would they send Lippy to the chair for killing his own boss?

If they did, it was okay by me. For although I knew that Lippy hadn't done it either, I certainly wasn't going to give away a usually respectable citizen to save a knife-throwing little rat like Lippy! He deserved to die!

Now that Iris Van Woden couldn't be indicted for the crime my conscience was clear—I felt I could safely hold my tongue and let the police blunder about in their usual slap happy fashion.

Edmond seemed to think so, too. He said: "So you didn't tell, after all."

"No—I didn't have time. But I think what's happened lets me out, doesn't it?"

"I guess it does at that. You sure you wouldn't like to let me know who really did kill Spagliotti? Was it Lippy?"

"You figure it for yourself, now, Edmond," I told him. "All I want to do is to wash my hands of the whole affair. Please don't let's talk about it anymore!" He nodded, and let the whole thing drop.

We went back to my apartments, and I asked him up for a drink. He said he didn't mind, so we took the elevator, and went up to my rooms. I opened the door, which I had not locked when we had left earlier, and we went in. I switched on the lights...

"Been waiting for you," said Lippy, training his gun on us from an easy chair. "Gotta little matter I wants to talk over with you!"

"Put that rod up, Lippy," snapped Edmond. "Before I get nasty about things!"

Lippy sneered. "Don't try the big stunts again, like you did yesterday, Mister Ross. This time I got a gun—an' I won't think twice before using it. Sit down, please!"

Edmond shrugged and nodded to me. We sat down facing the undersized little knifeman, waiting for him to start and ask us whatever he meant to ask us. He said: "You been down to the station, yes?"

"Yes."

"You know all about Iris Van Woden? She make a statement yes?"

"Yes—she made one of those, just a short while ago!"

Lippy's eyes shifted uneasily. "What she say?"

Edmond threw back his head and laughed like the dickens. "Scared, Lippy? Frightened she told them who really killed Spagliotti?"

"No, I'm not scared of that. I'm worried in case she told 'em who she thought killed Spagliotti—it wasn't me, no sir. Did she mention me at all?"

"She surely did, but plenty! In fact, before tonight's out I expect you'll be picked up for murder!"

Lippy drew breath in with a sharp hissing sound. "She told 'em about the letters?"

"Everything—about you being up there in the apartment, and all the rest of it."

Lippy bit his lower lip, said: "I thought she would—but I didn't have nothing to do with it. While I was sneaking down the alley leading to the kitchens, I spot a dame sneaking up—I don't see her face, on account she got it veiled. But she is some class, judging by her figures, which is A-Okay. I don't know where she'd been, or what doing, but never do I think it is the dame which I later know murdered the boss.

"When I gets up to the apartment in the lift, there is all quietness about, and lying there is the boss, with three bullets in his dome. I think I will get the letters anyways, but when I try

54

the combination, I find he has altered it. Then I see if Iris Van Woden is still up there, for I am not sure that she is not the skirt which I sees down below.

"I finds her in the clothes closet, and lets her out. She is plenty shook up, but I can see she does not believe my story that I see another dame sneaking away down the alley. She thinks that I killed the boss to get the letters. I warn her to keep shut her mouth and put her in a cab...but now she had to talk, yes!"

"That's so—but she'll do no more talking!"

"Eh?"

"Mean to say you don't know?"

"Know? I don't know anything. What happened?"

"Oh, nothing much! Just that your precious pal Mugs went and knocked off the dame with a Tommy gun, in full view of three witnesses. I fancy he hoped to kill us all, but he failed! So, you weren't in on that?"

Lippy looked very startled. He spluttered: "Geeze, no! I been waiting here for the best part of the night. Mugs said he is going to knock off that dame, and he goes out in the car with Lefty… I tell them I do not feel so hot, so's I can come here and see you. So, he does it! He is nuts, that Mugs. He gets so mad, he don't know what he is doing!"

"Mad's right—I guess this job's about the last he ever will do! He'll fry for this, see if he doesn't!"

Lippy stood up and moved towards the door, his beady eyes fixed on us. "I gotta go, now. Don't move until I get clear, or I don't hesitate to shoot. I got a place where the police'll never finds me—"

Edmond made a movement, and the frightened gangster menaced him sharply with his revolver. "I told you to keep still, don't I? You want to get a hot lead filling? Okay then—don't move!"

He transferred the door key to the outside, slid through the door and turned the key after him. We heard his feet racing towards the lift, then Edmond was throwing his weight against the door, trying to burst it open.

"No use," I sighed. "You'll never break that door down. It's solid oak, and the lock's made to last..."

"But damn it, we can't let the skunk get away! The cops may never get him!"

I beckoned him to the window and said: "This looks down into the street. You'll be able to see him from here, if he uses the front exit. Then it's up to you. While you're doing that, I'll call room service." I did so and asked them to send someone up to let us out.

"There he is," grated Edmond, suddenly. I rushed back to the window, peered out, and saw Lippy halt in indecision on the sidewalk. Then Edmond had his gun out, was aiming carefully at the small figure below.

"I'll try and just wing him," he explained. He pulled the trigger. Lippy jumped, and for a moment I thought he had been hit. But no, he glanced up; face white and terrified, then started to race across the street.

He was so busy thinking of us, he didn't see the big truck until he had dashed right in front of it. The driver had no chance to apply the brakes. We heard Lippy scream, just once, then the truck had gone clear over him, leaving a nasty mess on the roadway...a mess which had once been Lippy.

CHAPTER 7

MUGS GETS TOUGH

We went right down to the station again, told the Inspector what had occurred. He nodded at us, said: "Well, I guess that kind of closes the Spagliotti case, altogether, huh?"

I don't need to say I sighed with sheer relief. It had been on my mind ever since Iris Van Woden had been shot, that the Inspector would ask me just what I had been going to tell him about the murderer. Seemingly he took it for granted that now the killing had definitely been pinned on Lippy, there was no need for me to answer questions anymore. I really was glad of that—you'll know why, a little later.

Edmond made no reference to the real killer again; he, too, was contented to let it go at Lippy, and I didn't encourage him to ask any awkward questions.

I slept easily that night for the first time since the gang boss had gone the way of all flesh. My mind was free from worry, and as far as Mugs was concerned, that was another matter, and it was my firm intention, first thing in the morning, to ask to be taken off crime reporting—that's the way I felt. One murder had sickened me of it. Whether Claxon would see his way clear to fix it for me to get back to baby shows and social functions remained to be seen.

I woke early, about eight, had breakfast and dressed. I got down to the office about nine-thirty, and Claxon had gone off duty. But it was no use my hoping any longer that he'd take me off crime stuff: there was a memo waiting, assigning me to the Mugs case. I had to keep in touch with the vast manhunt which was going on and see if I could pick up any hot news.

I went along to Headquarters and hung around. Reports came in, but all were negative. Mugs seemed to have forsaken his usual haunts: probably he was well aware that the Sergeant,

Edmond and myself had seen him working that Thompson, and he knew there were sufficient witnesses to send him hell-for-leather towards getting the seat of his prison pants singed.

I might have known that he'd try something—but like a blind fool, I never thought he'd try what he did.

It happened after I'd reached home that night. I hadn't fixed any date with Edmond, and I had decided to have a quiet evening at home with a copy of *Liberty*. I thought I needed one after the way things had been sizzling lately. Accordingly, I settled down in the deep chair, stuck my feet on a buffet, and buried my nose in the mag. Within six minutes I was completely asleep.

It was the phone that woke me again. It seemed that I was fated to be annoyed by that phone. I was so mad I almost tore the connections loose; I thought it was Claxon, handing me another rush job. But it wasn't...

"Hello? Miss Curzon, speaking."

The voice from the other end was low and husky, as if the speaker were trying to whisper into the mouthpiece, and yet make himself clearly heard. He said: "This is Ross—Edmond Ross. Is that you, Anita?"

"Why yes, what's wrong, Edmond?"

"Plenty—I went out shooting trouble, and trouble's shot me! I can't explain over the phone, but I need fifty bucks urgently. Could you bring me that much over immediately?"

"But—"

"Don't but—I tell you it's a first priority. Or would you like to see me in a wooden casket, under six feet of earth, and five bunches of pansies?"

"I'll bring it. Edmond—where are you?"

"The address is Morton Avenue, off 25th, number five hundred and twenty. It's an empty house, but you'll find me there. Just walk up the path, and in at the door—I'll leave it open. And for God's sake don't spill this to anyone—if the cops knew what I'd done I'd be in an awful jam!"

"But Edmond—"

"Fifty bucks, kid, and hurry. I'll tell you all about it when you get here!" He hung up there, without telling me anything more.

With my head in a whirl, I rummaged in my workbox for the fifty dollars, found it, stuffed it in my bag, and shot out. On the way down I crammed my hat on hastily and rubbed a little lipstick over my lips.

I picked up a taxi at the corner, directed the driver to the address which Edmond had given me. We bowled along through Times Square and cut out into the quieter streets, heading towards the shadier neighborhoods. I wondered if Edmond had been gambling and lost heavily—or had he done something for which someone was blackmailing him?

These were questions which would soon be answered, anyway.

The taxi dropped me at the right address, and I paid off the driver, who looked curiously at me as I began to walk along the drive towards the apparently deserted house. It stood in its own grounds, and was a massive, rambling old mansion, which might have been built about the time that Washington was President. It was mainly composed of wood and was undoubtedly an eyesore on the face of the city. I wondered why no one had ever taken the trouble to pull it down. The windows were all broken and boarded up with wood-rotted planks; half the front steps were smashed through, and I had to tread very carefully to dodge going through under the porch.

As Edmond had said, the door was ajar; matter of fact, it couldn't have been any other way, for the rusty hinges had long since given up any hopes they might have entertained of holding the door in position and were now hanging crazily from two massive screws.

I cautiously pushed the door out of the way and stepped inside. The place was in darkness; not a sound broke into the stillness. From without, far away, as if in some other plane, came the muted rumble of traffic, and a million and one city noises, which one never notices until the circumstances are right. I felt lonely, and, I admit, a little frightened. I wished that Edmond would show up.

I called, softly: "Edmond—Ed! Are—are you here?"

There was no reply.

"Edmond." I called, a little louder. "Don't act the fool—tell me where you are."

Still no answer.

Now I was getting panicky. A cold fear was clutching at me, warning me to turn and run before it was too late. I half turned towards the door again, but the thought that possibly Edmond might be lying somewhere, injured, and too weak to shout, made me pause.

And as I stood there in indecision, in the darkness behind me, I heard the door slam! The breath rushed from my throat in a terrified gasp, and I whirled round, staring wildly into the gloom.

I could see nothing. Impenetrable darkness shrouded the long disused hallway; even the faint glimmer of starlight was now cut off from me. How long I stood there frozen, I have no idea. Perhaps ten minutes—perhaps only ten seconds. But at last, I fumbled in my bag with nervous fingers and brought out my lighter.

I flipped the thumb lever and was rewarded by a feeble glimmer. It wasn't very much use; hardly penetrated six feet into the black emptiness before me. I called, louder now: "Edmond—if you're playing some silly trick, stop it—my nerves won't stand it—Edmond! Oh, God, why don't you answer?"

"He can't answer, lady," mumbled a thick voice, and into the light from my lighter stepped Mugs! Mugs, with that horrible face of his leering at me in that glimmering, yellowish flame, and his great, knuckly hands reaching out towards me...

"Get away from me, you—you beast—don't touch me!" I shrilled.

He grinned stupidly and continued to come towards me—I wished desperately I had some kind of weapon, but I hadn't even a penknife. Wait a minute—I had a long—very long—nail file in my bag!

Desperately I fumbled for it, my eyes on the slowly, silently advancing gangster. I felt my fingers close about it, and dragged it from my bag, pointed end towards Mugs. I was violently afraid of him—I could see he had gone right off the deep end—not that he had ever been entirely sane, but now, the evil light in his eyes betrayed the fact that the killer in him reigned—that his brutal, primeval mind was lusting to torture and hurt...

"Stay away," I said, faintly. "I'll—I'll use this!"

I held it before his eyes, tightly, sick and faint from the horror which clutched at me. He simply grinned, idiotically, and continued to advance.

He was within two feet of me when I struck!

I struck for his eyes, hoping to damage one of them and give myself sufficient time to escape. I missed, for he jerked his head back, and the sharp point of the nail file punctured his flabby jowls.

A roar of pain came from him, and he went berserk. His heavy-shod foot drew back, came forward, catching me a crack on the knee. I screamed in agony and dropped the nail file in order to clutch my throbbing leg. It felt as if the bone was broken, and as I sobbed in anguish, Mugs kicked again, his foot smashing home on the hand which was clutching my knee. The pain was too much for me...

61

I felt the hallway whirling round me and tried to see Mugs to dodge his foot if he kicked again. But my lighter was out, and pitch darkness was all around me.

He did kick again, and as I was now on my knees, the kick took me shatteringly in the chest...

I seemed to hear a thousand banshees wailing, through my haze of pain, and realized it was merely myself screaming... Then a merciful curtain of blackness fell over my mind...

*   *   *   *

I came round after an interminable period of wandering in an inky void, being pursued by gangsters, armed with Tommy guns and pendulous lower lips. Dozens of policemen were there, also, trying to out-shout each other as to who should have the pleasure of third-degreeing me.

It was a horrible dream, but not so horrible as the reality when I awoke. I was still in the empty house: I knew that by the dust and the moldering stench of rotting wallpaper; by the dust-coated window to the right. There were two guttering candles burning in a shabby holder and revealing the rest of the scene to my eyes.

Mugs was there, and Lefty.

And so was the sergeant from the police station, and Edmond!

The sergeant appeared to be unconscious, but Edmond was gazing at me with pity in his eyes.

The breaths I took were almost rattling into my lungs. My chest wheezed painfully at each, and I was aware of a dull, throbbing pain down my left side. I felt, with a sickly feeling, that some of my ribs had caved in under Mugs' last kick. And, as I found later, they had. Two, to be exact.

Edmond said: "Tough luck, kid! How'd they get you here?"

"I—I—oh!" I stopped, as a sudden pang shot through me.

"Hurt badly?" asked Edmond.

I nodded, silently. I managed to say: "I thought you phoned me and asked me to come on here..."

"I see—the old gag...too bad you fell for it. You might have known..."

"How did they get you?" I queried, looking at the nasty, blood-smeared cut in his forehead.

"Me? Well, I was as big a mug as you were. I had a call, purporting to come from a prospective client. He asked me to come down here, and like a sap I did. The rest was easy. I think they got the sergeant there much the same way. Only they hit him too hard..."

"I know—I see he hasn't yet regained consciousness!"

"He won't either. He's dead!"

I shuddered, said: "But why have they done all this?"

"Surely you can twig that?"

"You mean that—because we three were witnesses to the shooting at headquarters?"

"That's it in a nutshell. Once we three are dead, the State won't be able to prosecute—at least, without us they won't actually have an eyewitness, and some crooked lawyer will get Mugs off. You know how it goes!"

I knew how it went, all right. And I swore at myself for coming down here, being taken in by the oldest trick imaginable. I swore very hard, but silently, and I called myself some very unladylike names. Then the pain of my chest took my thoughts away from my foolishness, and I lay there and gasped weakly.

Mugs and Lefty were doing something in the corner. They had a pile of old papers there, and they were spreading a can of kerosene over them. The pungent smell permeated the room and made me feel sicker than ever. The job done, Mugs straightened and came towards us.

"Here's where youse folks get a one-way trip." He grinned, his big lump of a face nauseatingly simple, except for the murder lamps in his eyes. And it wasn't 'til then that I knew what he meant to do—he meant to burn us to death, together with that old house!

CHAPTER 8

IT ALWAYS HAPPENS TO KILLERS

I realized Mugs' intentions. I also realized that we wouldn't stand a chance of rescue or escape, before the dry timbers of that old house had blazed to ashes—taking us with them. No doubt the hook-and-ladder boys would get to the blaze in good time, but they certainly wouldn't be soon enough to save us, trapped in the room which was to be the seat of the fire.

Mugs leered down at us. He was taking no chances with Edmond—he clutched a large revolver in one hand. Edmond gazed at this and sneered: "The Complete Gangster!"

"Shut it," snarled Mugs, aiming a sickening kick at Edmond's head. He rolled rapidly aside, and the foot succeeded only in catching the detective's shoulder.

"What's wrong with shooting us?" remarked Edmond, coolly. "Is it too quick, or something?"

"It ain't that—I don't wanna leave any traces of where you birds have gone—you're just gonna vanish, and I reckon you'll do that okay when this joint gets cooking."

"An' then there'll be no eyewitnesses to testify against you if ever you do get picked up?"

"That's the size of it, smart dick. I wouldn't have needed to go to all this trouble if you hadn't spotted me in time and ducked, the other night at Headquarters!"

"Go ahead," jeered Edmond. "They'll get you, someday, Mugs! An' when they do, and they've put you on the hot squat, just remember that I'll be waiting, down there for you...."

Mugs shrugged, turned to Lefty. "Ready?"

"Okay, boss!"

Mugs struck a match and flipped it on to the paper. The kerosene roared into sudden life, and almost immediately the dried wood which the flames were licking commenced to crackle.

Mugs looked at us, grinned, and with Lefty close behind him, left the building. We gazed with horror at the door which they had jammed shut. Edmond said: "Keep your face as close the ground as you can—maybe you'll last longer that way. I've been turning a plan over in my noggin since I saw what he meant to do—now I'll try it!"

"What—what is it?"

"We're on the second floor, here. Over in that far corner, all the wooden flooring is half rotten. If I can smash through the ceiling underneath and fall to the floor, I may be able to roll right out of the house—they can't have closed the front door, on account of its falling off its hinges. And if I can get as far as the street, I'll be able to bring help. Hang on, kid, and hope for the best."

He had rolled over to the weakest part of the floor, and was jerking frantically into the air, allowing his hard heels to smash down on the old boarding. I tore my eyes away from the side of the room opposite which was now a sheet of flame. I prayed that Edmond would succeed, and, if so, that he wouldn't break his neck when he took the drop, bound hand and foot, into the room beneath!

I could have cheered when I heard the sharp crack and a splinter of the wood giving way under his determined assault. He strained his head over his shoulder, grinned, and said: "Here I go—wish me luck, honey!"

Then he had rolled directly on top of the gap he had made, and had slid down between two stout beams, and started kicking at the fragile ceiling of the room beneath. I heard the roof cave in, heard the thud of his body hitting the room below. Then silence...

I was so numb with pain now, that I didn't even have the strength to pray any longer. I just lay, watching the flames

66

racing nearer, coughing harsh, rasping coughs, as the acrid fumes tore into my lungs.

I thought of rolling over to the hole Edmond had made, but when I tried the pangs of agony in my chest made me feel sick and helpless and I lay still. The flames were scorching my clothing and I had resigned myself as best I could to the fate which seemed to be in store, when there was a crashing on the closed door. I was practically unconscious through the thick black smoke which swirled about the room, but I managed a weak cry: "Edmond!"

I felt strong arms about me, and was lifted and carried rapidly across the floor, on to the landing, down the stairs, and into the cool night air. I looked up and saw I was in the brawny arms of a blue uniformed patrolman. I whispered: "Edmond—did he...did he get out? Did he tell you?"

"Sure, he's all right," assented the policeman. "He rolled out right in front o' me feet an' says you are back up there. He broke a leg, but otherwise I fancy he's okay!"

I think I managed one short sigh of relief. Then the pain, and the pressure of events, took their toll of me, and I passed right out cold...

*   *   *   *

They got Mugs and Lefty, and on our testimony they both went to the chair one chilly September morning. And so, the Spagliotti murder case was entirely concluded; and if the world was minus one gangster, one society girl, and three rats nobody cared much, except perhaps the girl's parents.

I spent two months in hospital, and Edmond spent one. Then, naturally, we got married. I gave up newspaper reporting.

It was about two weeks after our marriage, just after we had returned from our honeymoon (and what a honeymoon!), when Detective-Inspector Flannel dropped in on us in our brand new apartment. Edmond was seated before a leaping fire, in dressing gown and slippers, strewing the new carpet with cigarette ash. I was sitting opposite—er—knitting a—well, if you must know, knitting a little something for another little something we hoped one day would arrive.

Flannel stood with his back to the fire, warming his hands. Finally, he reached in the pocket of his stroller, brought out a small parcel. "Sorry I didn't get to the wedding," he remarked, "but there was something of a rush down at Headquarters. Anyway, I brought along a small gift…"

I thanked him and opened the package eagerly. Inside was another paper wrapper. I opened this and two books fell out.

"One," said Flannel, with a grin, "is for your husband. One's for you!"

I looked at them. They were: How to Be a Good Reporter and First Steps in Private Detecting!

Flannel grinned as he saw our expressions. Then he said: "No, seriously, my present will be delivered tomorrow. I got hold of a swell ice box."

"This is most unexpected, Inspector."

"Not really—you two were a help on the Spagliotti case! Mind you, you needn't think I'm blind. I happen to be sure that Lippy didn't do any killing—not as far as his boss was concerned."

I was sitting bolt upright, looking at him with a peculiar expression. He didn't meet my eyes—just gazed over our heads through the window at the winking city lights. He said: "Here's the way it really went. I couldn't get over those gloves we found! And then, Miss Curzon, you seemed to be holding something back, continually. Also, you knew a great deal about the crime. So, I started to investigate a little: I found out that once upon a time Spagliotti moved out west in order to lie low for a spell. He went to a small dump called Middleville in the mid-western States, and there he led the life of a normal citizen for a time. Out there, too, was a seventeen-year-old girl. Unlike most of her age, she didn't go for swoon crooners—no, this dame was a bobby-soxer for gangsters, real tough guys! She thought they were all like Humphrey Bogart, James Cagney and George Raft; thought they all had a better side. She was wrong, but she didn't know that!

"Unknown to her folks, she started visiting this Spagliotti at the lodge he had hired. She was a silly kid, and there could only be one end to a thing like that—and it happened that way! Spagliotti blew town, when he was ready, leaving her three months pregnant! She drowned herself in the local swimming hole. They found her one Sunday morning and brought her home. In her pocket was a letter, telling how, when and who!

"Her elder sister, a young lady by the name of Estelle Hargreaves, had seen Spagliotti round the town. She was working on a small-town paper, but soon she managed to get a New York appointment. She hadn't wanted to go to New York, not until that had happened to her kid sister. But then she decided that rats like Spagliotti shouldn't live! She came here, waited her chance. Nobody knew her as Estelle Hargreaves...she had taken a pen name...the name of...."

He stopped here and looked directly at me. There were tears in my eyes, from the memory of the tragedy he had just recalled.

I wiped them dry, said:

"You're right, Inspector! I killed Spagliotti!"

He nodded, said: "You planned it all well, didn't you? But you made your mistake when you took your gloves off to wash the blood from your hands; blood which you had got there by kneeling to see if you really had killed him!

"You were so panicky you forgot the gloves! You remembered this on the way down, isn't that right? And you took good care to wipe any prints you might have left from the dumb waiter. But you weren't aware that we now have a method by which fingerprints can be taken from materials I suspected you already, you seemed so tied up with the case and I didn't have much trouble getting a set of your prints—and they matched!

"That was before I pinned the killing on Lippy. After Iris Van Woden had told us her story, accusing Lippy, you were about to speak...but if you think back, you'll remember that I stopped you before you could confess. I didn't wish anyone else to hear—I had already found out why you murdered the man, and I didn't see any harm in letting Lippy take the rap for it. That's why I discredited his story of having seen some woman leaving the hotel as he was going. I may be a fool, but...."

I gasped. "Then—then you aren't—you aren't going to arrest me?"

"Why should I? Ordinarily you're a peaceable citizen. Can't say I blame you for killing Spagliotti—I don't blame you! Nope, I'm keeping it under my lid, and I'd advise you to do the same."

Edmond stood up, gripped the Inspector's hand. He said:

"You're a sport, Inspector. I really didn't know it was Anita—or shall I say Estelle. She didn't tell me, but now I do know, all I can say about it is that I'm twice as proud of having Anita for my wife..."

Flannel smiled, accepted the drink which Edmond poured out for him. He raised his glass, said: "Here's to a quiet week..."

At which point the phone rang again. Edmond answered it, held it towards Flannel. He said: "Headquarters—for you!"

Flannel took it, listened.

"What! Vanity Stevens, the strip-tease star? Murdered? In her dressing room at the Follies Theatre? Sure. I'll be right over... Nope, don't let one solitary damned reporter in—tell 'em to scram till later. They won't? They will when I get there..."

He slammed down the phone, settled his hat on his head, said: "Vanity Stevens the strip-teaser has just been found with her lily-white throat sliced! Here's your chance, Mrs. Ross, like to come along and see? I'll give you an exclusive."

I shuddered and said: "No thanks, Inspector, you can have it all! The Spagliotti case was enough to finish me for the rest of my life—I don't want any more broken ribs!"

He grinned, said a hasty so-long, and flew through the door like a tornado. We could hear him buzzing impatiently for the elevator.

Edmond smiled, came over and sat beside me. I said to him: "Well, now you know at last."

"Yeah, honey, now I know. Funny thing, it was as plain as the nose on my face that you'd had a hand in the killing somehow, yet I never suspected you! I guess I'm a pretty poor detective when it comes to brains!"

I said: "Brains don't always count, Edmond. Not unless you have the courage to back them up with—and you certainly have that!"

He grinned: "I bet you say that to all your husbands!"

"What do you think of your wife now? Aren't you ashamed to have a wife who's committed murder?"

"I sure am," he said. "I hate my wife having to work—so, in future, if you feel like killing anybody, don't! Just tell me— I'll do it for you, honey!"

THE END

THE EGYPTIAN TOMB

CHAPTER 1

TWO MEN IN MASKS

I paused at the corner of my street which led to the house where I maintained bachelor apartments and glanced back furtively.

They were still there, those two men in masks, some way in the rear, but dimly visible under the feeble rays of a streetlamp.

I felt a twinge of apprehension and hurried onwards. The two men in masks followed swiftly....

Perhaps I should explain something about myself: my name is Tony Gilmour—and I was, until last month, a practicing member at the Bar. Then I was unceremoniously kicked out of my profession for presenting false evidence in court on behalf of a client. Of course, I hadn't any idea it was false evidence, but the powers that be thought otherwise—so there I was, a promising career nipped in the bud, with hardly more than a few hundred in the bank, and unfitted for any employment other than that which I had lost.

I hadn't worried much; rather the reverse. I'd driven the whole affair out of my mind and concentrated on doing nothing but enjoying myself for a full month. But the month was up and now I had been forced to think about obtaining other employment.

My parents were dead, and the only relative I owned, Uncle Emery, was as hard and gritty as his name implies, and would scarcely bother his head to any extent about me even if I had approached him. Of course, he might have given me a job in his shipping office, but unfortunately shipping offices had never exercised any great appeal.

I had been downtown looking in the wanted ads in the newspapers at my club, the Meridian. I hadn't found anybody who wanted to engage a chap of my peculiar talents, and, as it was growing dark rapidly, being January, I had left the club and

75

started to walk home to my apartments, not being in the position to afford a taxi, and not being partial to tram cars or buses.

And then I had become aware of the two men in masks, some distance behind, but undoubtedly following me.

The district I live in is pretty deserted at ten o'clock at night, especially so when it is a crisp, cold January night. And there was no trace of a moon in the sky. But I had heard their footsteps echoing after me along the deserted streets, and when they had begun to turn all the corners I had turned, I had stolen a glance back. Under the rays of a lamp had seen two men in dark coats, their hats pulled well down over their eyes, and, just visible under the hats, black masks.

I hurried my steps a little, a feeling of impending trouble fastening on to my mind. The two men hurried their steps in time with my own.

I kept an eye open for a police constable on the way, but it is a remarkable fact that when you desire the presence of a limb of the law in London, they are usually remarkably conspicuous by their non-appearance. And so, with my two followers not far in the rear, I reached my own apartments.

I hurried up the stairs, paused at my room door to listen. Sure enough, within a few seconds, two pairs of steps sounded on the narrow staircase; two dark trilbys hove into view on the landing below.

I entered my room quickly, moved rapidly over to my desk. I jerked open the top drawer, slid my hand inside, and brought out a Colt automatic. It was one which I had kept handy ever since I had secured a conviction against a certain 'Idler' Brooks, a criminal of the lowest type, but reputed to have several friends who would avenge the long term of imprisonment he had received on the man who had been responsible for him receiving it. I flipped back the safety catch...

I hadn't bothered to switch on the lights: I edged back in the darkness behind the door, held the revolver ready...

I must admit I am not a good shot. But I was counting on their blindness when entering to give me the proverbial element of surprise.

The door of my room opened cautiously; a head was inserted, and a voice whispered: "It's all right, come on! He must be in bed!"

"So soon?" queried the other man, his voice low and hoarse.

"Well, anyway, he isn't in here. Come on in...."

The two of them ventured entirely into the room, walked over to the desk and stood there, seemingly undecided. At that moment I slammed the door and flicked on the lights!

The two intruders jumped in surprise; their eyes popping under their black masks they spun round and stared at me as if they could hardly believe what they saw.

"All right," I smiled grimly, advancing a little, my gun wavering menacingly towards their chests, "—now let's hear all about it! I suppose you're a couple of 'Idler' Brooks' pals?"

I was entirely unprepared for their next action. As if moved by a common mechanism, they both opened their mouths wide and yelled with merriment.

"If that isn't the limit," laughed the tallest. "Here we come along to play a joke on old Tony, and blessed if he doesn't turn the tables!"

"You may consider it a joke," I informed them mirthlessly, "but I don't think the police will! Will one of you be good enough to pick up that phone and dial Whitehall 1212—I think that is the usual procedure, isn't it?"

"Here, hang on," gulped the tall one, suddenly losing his mirth, "do you mean to tell us you don't know us, Tony?"

"Am I supposed to?" I asked.

"Of course you are, man! Here, Alan, take your mask off before the ass takes a pot at us...!"

Between spasms of laughter, they removed their masks, and I almost staggered when their features were revealed to me, for I knew them well enough now! They were my old Oxford friends Alan Glenhaven and Ron Everest.

Seeing them like this bought back a rush of those distant memories which had lain neglected at the back of my subconscious mind. Those glorious days at Oxford: the riotous study rags, the gravity of the lecture rooms, the solemnity of the Cloisters, the quaintness of the old town and the awful suspense of graduation day.

"You're a par of damned fools!" I grunted, "Why, anything might have happened! Suppose I'd shot first and asked questions afterwards?"

"Sorry, Tony," Alan smiled ruefully, "we'd no idea you were an armed desperado! Absolutely none at all!"

"Perhaps we were rather rash," smiled Ron, stepping forward and pumping my hand up and down. "We spotted you in the club and couldn't resist playing a joke on you. We intended to follow you home, then try to scare you by telling you we'd come to bump you off. But it seems you've got the laugh on us after all!"

I invited them to sit down, and I brought out a bottle of whisky and a siphon. Soon we were exchanging old reminiscences and roaring with laughter. Then they asked how I was getting along, and rather shamefacedly I told them.

"But look here," said Ron, his voice excited, "that means that you're free, doesn't it? I mean you haven't any commitments here in England, have you? Nothing to hold you here?"

"I'm afraid not—not at the moment," I assented.

"Why, that's wonderful, then! You can come along with Alan and me to Egypt!"

I stared at them blankly, watching the enthusiasm in both their faces.

"Yes, he must," Alan nodded. "The three of us together again! How about it, Tony?"

"Hang on," I admonished, sternly, "I don't even know what you idiots are talking about yet. What's all this about Egypt? And who's in the party? And what does the party propose to do in Egypt?"

"It's like this, Tony," Ron said, turning in my direction. "Perhaps you know Alan's father was an Egyptologist? Remember when we used to go along to Glenhaven Towers for the holidays and used to muck about with all those old mummy cases and bits of Egyptian pottery and stuff?...You do? Good! Well, Alan's father met with an accident last year while he was excavating in some spot midway between El Bawiti and Farafra Oasis. Apparently, a section of the tomb he was exploring collapsed on him and he was killed instantly.

"We don't know if he had expected anything of this sort, but strangely enough he had given his Dragoman—not long before his accident—a letter to post in Cairo. It was addressed to Alan here. I happened to be down at Glenhaven Towers for a stay when the letter arrived, and it quite upset Alan at first when he learned that his father had been—well, accidentally killed!

"But when we'd read the letter, it began to look as if the death hadn't been so accidental as people thought. In fact, after we'd scrutinized the whole affair from all angles, we were both almost convinced that his father had been—murdered!"

Here he glanced sympathetically at Alan, who said: "Go on. If Dad's dead, there's no use in not talking things over. Any feelings I had about the matter were eased down long since. Tell Tony what was in the letter! You've got it on you, haven't you?"

Ron extracted his wallet and took from it an envelope. He opened this and took out a thick white sheet of notepaper on which was written closely crammed lines of ragged pencilled scrawl. He began to read in a low voice:

"'My dear son, I am writing this seated on a slab of granite which the native workers have just uprooted from the Tomb of Ko Len Tep, an ancient Egyptian High Priest.

"'As you should know, this tomb I am excavating was located from the records of Penshepa, whose mummy now reposes in my own private museum at Glenhaven Towers. Therefore, the entire credit of this find goes to me alone, and I have hopes of discovering something really worthwhile—and, in addition, a great deal of wealth: gems, gold, trophies, etc., which, according to the records of Penshepa, were buried with Ko Len Tep, who was not only a High Priest but a man of great worldly wealth!

"'However, I feel this is beside the point, for I am the only one who is aware of what was buried with the priest. No, there is something else, something very strange going on about here. When we found the tomb—only the shallowest layer of sand covered the entrance—and it's obvious that a tomb which has lain untouched in a waste of sand which is continually shifting should have been well buried by now. Of course, it is possible that the last shift of the sand dunes served to bring the tomb entrance as we found it, within a foot of the top of the sand. But again, I think not!

"'Besides that, and the usual legend about death befalling anyone who desecrates the resting places of ancient Egypt (which is mere rot!), there have been a number of strange accidents about the place. Men have been killed while at work, and others have been injured. Today, not half an hour ago, the whole bunch of them deserted en masse! All except my dragoman, an Egyptian called Mustapha and various other names which I forget, they are so numerous. It is all very strange, and I have the feeling that someone—but I don't know who, or why—wishes to prevent me entering further into the tomb!

"'I, myself, have suffered two narrow escapes: one from the bullets of a gang of Bedouins who attacked the camp and whom we drove off without much trouble, and the other from a mysterious assailant who attacked me with a knife one evening after I had retired, but only succeeded in wounding me slightly.

"'However, I still have an uneasy feeling that something may happen. Accordingly, I am writing this letter which I shall give to Mustapha to post in Cairo if I, myself, fail to return there.

"'Whatever happens I mean to go on excavating! I think that now I have discovered the means of operating the outer door it will not be long before the inner door falls to me also, and I shall then be able to enter the burial chambers proper... If anything should go wrong, Alan, I want you to investigate, for there is undoubtedly more here than meets the eye!

"'I trust sincerely that there will be no necessity to send this letter... But should you ever receive it, try to obtain permission to complete my excavations and do so... I've always thought you've got the right stuff in you...

"'Just in case you do receive this letter, so long, and remember we were always close...'"

Here Ron broke off. Glancing towards Alan, I knew from his face that the death had hit him harder than he cared to acknowledge, for there had always been, I recalled, a sort of friendly camaraderie between Alan and his Professor father. I had often envied him that easy relationship.

"As far as we can gather," went on Ron, slowly, "the Professor ventured into the tomb alone the following day. Whether he succeeded in opening the inner door we don't know, but the dragoman Mustapha said he was returning towards the exit with his face showing considerable excitement when the entire ceiling collapsed on him! By the time Mustapha had managed to drag him out he was already...dead.

"There was an investigation, but the cause of death was put down as misadventure, and the matter, as far as the Egyptian authorities were concerned, was closed! But it wasn't as far as Alan and myself were concerned! We applied for permission to continue excavations—and received it, provided we realized the danger attached to the affair. For the tomb, they told us, was obviously in a state of collapse, and possibly there would be more accidents."

We were all silent for a moment, then Alan said: "So that's it! And next week we're off to the land of the inscrutable Sphinx..."

They both turned towards me, and as one man, said: "How about it, Tony?" and Alan added: "Expenses are on the house, and if we find any treasure there'll be a three-way split... Will you come?"

"Will I?" I smiled, gripping their hands in turn. "Just you try and stop me!"

CHAPTER 2

EGYPT

Morning! And rising in the distance, beyond the turgid Nile-yellow waters of the sea, I could discern a long, low shoreline. Egypt! To be more precise, Alexandria; but a less romantic terrain than that which now confronts us and towards which our ship is rapidly steaming, would be hard to imagine.

Under the dull light, rapidly taking shape, were steamers, sails, the squat outlines of warehouses, and factory chimneys, with only an odd, occasional minaret thrusting up against the rain-heavy sky.

Ron must have noticed my disappointment, for he gave a sympathetic grin and clapped me on the back. "Not so sunny and romantic as you thought, eh? Well, never mind! This is only Alexandria, and there's a whole lot more of Egypt than this, you know. We happen to be docking on a nasty kind of day but wait until we get as far as Cairo—then you'll really be able to see some of the mysterious East!"

"I am a bit disappointed," I admitted ruefully, "but I dare say one can't expect a modern port to be very—exotic!"

"I'm disappointed myself." grunted Alan. "I mean, this looks more or less like a lot of European ports I know. I'll be glad to get on to Cairo."

The ship rapidly drew in, and in another hour the three of us dressed in white drill, were quickly pushing our way through the crowds of beggars, guides, Arabs in flowing robes, Egyptians in sombre garments and European garb, but usually wearing a tarboosh (generally red), towards the station and the early morning train for Cairo. Alan and I would have liked to have lingered a little longer in this, the first city of Egypt we had ever seen, but Ron, who had been through all this before, wished to push on to Cairo.

83

"There's very little to see here," he told us. "The museum and possibly Pompey's Pillar, but these are nothing compared with the sights you'll get later on!"

And so we rushed on, catching only a brief glimpse of white stucco and brick houses, winding labyrinthine streets, and one or two ultra-modern boulevards. We took the train in good time, found it solid but uncomfortable. Before we had hardly regained our breath we were moving from the city, past suburbs of neat white villas, houses, native quarters of coarse mud huts, and finally into the open where our curious eyes dwelt on fields of bananas and figs. Soon came small patches of fertile land with growing crops, and now and then herds of cows, buffaloes and goats, tended by thin, brown sticks of natives.

The mast and sail of a felucca rises from the very ground in front of our astonished eyes, and Ron smilingly explained: "The rest of the boat is in a canal which we cannot see from here. As we go along the view won't be quite so depressing."

He is right. Shortly the countryside lifts upwards, out of the mire, and we stop at a filthy little mud village. From the window we could see swaying camels, black-robed women riding donkeys, and fellahin tending to herds of goats and brown sheep. This was the first real glimpse we had of Egypt— but it was, as Ron said, the flat land of the Delta and not the Egypt of the Nile Valley.

The train stopped at Damanhur and hordes of hawkers rushed towards it crying their wares, which bordered on almost everything. Red tarbooshes and gold braid were much in evidence on the station platform, and Ron told us these were not—as we had assumed—police officials, but merely railway officials directing the crowd of dismounting passengers.

Eventually we had reached Cairo itself and we found, much to our surprise, that the weather had miraculously cleared up, and the sun was beaming from a blue-clad sky on to the impressive mosques, minarets and swaying palms of the great

84

city. We were to stay here for three days, since we had decided that we might as well mix pleasure with our business, and three days, Ron said, was ample for all we should wish to see of Cairo.

We selected three of the dozen porters who pestered us for our luggage, and finally found ourselves piled into the taxi—an ancient and ramshackle affair which was to take us to our hotel. Ron had chosen the Savoy, which stands in the Sharia Kasr-el-Nil, near the English Consulate, and not far from Helouan Station at which we had arrived. We found the hotel spacious and clean and were quite comfortable in the rooms provided for us. After a hasty lunch, Alan and I were ready to take in some of the sights and Ron agreed to act as our guide.

But this was not to be, for as we stepped from the hotel exit a somewhat gaudily robed dragoman with a lean, brown skinned face walked across to us ingratiatingly and made a violent and eloquent bow in front of us. He then spoke in his own language, and Ron, who speaks the tongue fluently, answered for us. I was able to pick up the gist of his conversation myself, for I have dabbled from time to time in various foreign languages; and although I never succeeded in gaining complete mastery of any yet, I know sufficient of most to manage upon. Only Alan was unable to gather what the man was driving at.

"Lord," said the dragoman very eloquently, "my name is Mustapha Selim Hassan Mahmoud! I was dragoman to his late Lordship Professor Glenhaven. I understood from a communication I received from you that you would wish to engage me as your dragoman in your projected expedition?"

"So, you are Mustapha!" replied Ron, gravely.

"Mustapha Selim Hassan Mahmoud, Lord!"

"Hmm! Well, we can't call you all that. Mustapha will have to do!"

"What's the chap want, Ron?" Alan asked.

85

"He was your father's dragoman—Mustapha." He turned to the Egyptian. "My friend Alan here is your late master's child—the son of his heart, who has come to find that which his father left unfound."

A gleam of interest appeared in the man's eyes. He said: "This, then, is the lord who pays the money?"

"That is even he," smiled Ron.

The change in Mustapha was immediate and amazing. Turning to Alan, he displayed his white teeth in an immense smile, bowed low, and said in passable English: "Welcome to Cairo, master! I, Mustapha, will serve you faithfully and well, for was not your father a great man? And did not I, Mustapha Selim Hassan Mahmoud, hold for him a great love and respect! Sair, I am at your disposal! I, the greatest guide in all Cairo— the finest dragoman in all Egypt!"

"That's decent of you, Mustapha. I understand you have the map with the location of the Tomb of Ko Len Tep?"

The dragoman bowed again. "Even so, Lord. I, Mustapha, took it from your father's pocket as he lay dead in my arms. I have it hidden well, for it is a thing of great value."

"Where'd you learn to speak English so well?" asked Ron, curiously.

Mustapha smiled: "Sair, was I not dragoman to Professor Glenhaven for many, many years? He it was who taught me this."

"Look here," said Alan, eagerly, "how about forgetting the sights for today? Suppose we all have a look at this map of Mustapha's? Can you get it for us now?"

"At once, sair. If you will but accompany me to my humble residence I will acquire it for you immediately—or, if you prefer it, I will bring it to the hotel."

"We'll go with you," smiled Ron. "We came out for a walk, and we may as well have it. Lead on, oh Mustapha!"

Mustapha beamed with pleasure and led on.

As we followed, Ron explained to us the neighbourhood we had now entered. "This is known as the Muski," he began.

"That's how it smells, too," I said, wrinkling my nose up as various odours drifted out and assailed my nostrils from the quaint shops which lined the street.

"It's quite the place for trading—bazaars, curio shops, cafés, taverns and that sort of thing."

I glanced with interest at the many, mainly European-garbed, merchants, who stood before their shops trying to lure the unwary tourist inside to purchase rugs, silks, brasses, rare manuscripts and a million and one articles which were probably manufactured in a spot no more romantic than a modern factory.

We turned off this street into a narrower, dirtier one. "The Khan Khalili," Ron told us. "Here's where you really do get the real thing—sometimes! But you'll pay through the nose for it!"

In front of us, Mustapha was pushing his way through the crowds of robed figures which congested the street. He shouldered aside a plump, veiled woman carrying a fat child on her hip, and was rewarded by a hissed epithet. He turned into a doorway, which was little more than a crack in the wall, and we ascended some dark, noisome stairs to a tiny square room roughly furnished with old rugs and rickety divans, at the top.

Mustapha bade us be seated, and crossed to a small box in the corner, fumbling in his robes for the key. But as he knelt to unfasten the lock, a startled oath left his lips and he turned to us with an agitated countenance. "Sairs, the box has been forced open!"

"What!" Ron sprang forward and flipped back the iron lid of the stout box. The interior was devoid of anything but air. He stood up with a grim look in his eyes, turned to us, and said: "This seems more than a casual robbery to me! I've an idea this map was stolen by the same persons responsible for the Professor's death!"

"My God!" muttered Alan. "What do we do now?"

"Perhaps Mustapha can remember enough about the details of the map to guide us to the Tomb?" I suggested. We all turned to Mustapha, and he nodded.

"Yes, sairs. Mustapha remember all! He will guide you to the Tomb of Ko Len Tep! Have no fear, gentlemens."

Rather thoughtfully we followed him outside again, and he began to guide us back to the Savoy, where we planned to hold a sort of council of war. But as we were halfway back, I began to notice the woman following behind,

She had followed us to Mustapha's place, I was sure, for I recalled having noticed her on the way down. She was heavily veiled, clad in long, dark, typical robes, and a thick yashmak fell completely over her face from the bridge of the nose down. Only her eyes were visible, and these were dark, large, and mysterious.

We turned a corner, and whispering hastily to my surprised friends that there was some business I had to attend to, I cut off into a small shop. They paused, but from the shadowy doorway I signed to them to continue. They shrugged but did as they had been directed. I waited there, crouching back in the shadows; waited for the arrival of that mysterious shapeless figure which, something told me, was on our trail!

The touch of a light hand on my shoulder made me start with surprise. I spun round, to behold a fat, baggy-trousered brown gentleman, with a prominent nose. He was holding up for my admiring gaze a small stone tablet with hieroglyphics chiselled on it. "Behold," he said, enthusiastically, "is it not perfect?"

With my eyes glued to the corner, I said: "What is it?"

A note of hurt and surprise entered his voice. He sounded as if he were about to burst into tears. He said: "What is it? Does not the gentleman know? But it is the personal visiting card of Rameses the Second! The only one in existence! The

Museum have offered me five hundred piastres for it, but I do not care to sell to them, for I have great love of white people. So, sair, to you I will dispose of this priceless piece for—hmm!—fifty piastres!"

I shook my head, for I had suddenly glanced round the door and had seen the figure of the woman come into view, hurrying after my friends.

"Thirty piastres?" said the merchant.

"No, I think not."

"Twenty?"

Again, I shook my head.

"Ten piastres then? Come, noble sir, do not put upon a poor, ignorant merchant! You will ruin me! Eight piastres, and I can go no lower! Take it quickly, ere I change my mind and remember that it cost sixty piastres!"

"I'm sorry," I said, slowly, preparing to leave the shop in the wake of the woman shadow, "I'm afraid I don't care to buy anything today."

"You joke, sair," pleaded the merchant, his voice vibrating with emotion. "You still try to rob me! My, but you are hard men for a bargain, you English! Come, five piastres, and I will let my wife and fourteen children starve!"

"Sorry," I told him, stepping briskly from the shop after the retreating woman. "Some other time, perhaps. I merely stepped in out of the sun for a moment!"

"Mad!" I heard him mutter as I hurried away. "They are all mad, these Inglees! Bah! Infidels! I spit me of them! Stepped in out of the sun! Pah! 'tis in my mind that he did not step in soon enough…" And then I was out of earshot.

It was quite a procession back to the Savoy. The woman, if she had noticed my absence from the party, obviously did not for a second consider that she herself was now being trailed. She paused at the corner of the building, watched the others enter the hotel, then turned hurriedly and retraced her steps. I had to duck quickly into a narrow alcove to prevent her seeing me. With myself still close on her trail, she began to return the way she had come. Intrigued, and feeling that I was on the track of something which would perhaps throw light on the peculiar mystery surrounding the death of the professor and the theft of the map, I forgot time and place, and found myself walking through tortuous, twisted, winding thoroughfares, which became ever narrower and dirtier. But after a time, these began to vanish, and in their stead, majestic three-storied stucco houses rose towards the evening shadows, which were now rapidly lengthening across the dusty roads.

The woman turned into one of these, which stood in its own grounds and was surrounded by thick clusters of eucalyptus trees. After a hasty glance round, I followed her, experiencing no great difficulty in sliding through the wide gates, and under the friendly shade of the luxuriant trees. She made her way to a side door of the house and entered without the use of a key. Casting caution to the wind, I forgot any possibility of danger and moved silently after her. The door opened to my touch, and I stepped inside the house. It was quiet and deserted, and trying hard to stifle my breathing I crept forward in the darkness to a door, from under which shone the pallid rays of a lamp. I had bent, ready to peer through the keyhole, when something crushed on my skull with a stunning force...

CHAPTER 3

THE WOMAN IN THE CASE

I wasn't really knocked cold, I suppose; merely badly stunned: so badly that I couldn't see clearly for some minutes—so badly that I was only dimly aware of rough hands seizing me, of being dragged clumsily into the room I had been about to spy in. By the time I had fully recovered, my hands were bound behind my back, and I was lying slumped against the wall in one corner. The oil lamp had been turned out altogether and only the rays of a strong electric torch seared across the darkness, the white glare eating into my eyes so that to see at all I was forced to screw my lids down to narrow slits.

Whoever had hit me—and I felt sure that the woman I had trailed could not have struck so forcibly—must be behind that torch beam. But who were they? What were they? And what had the woman to do with all this?

Then the woman spoke. Her voice was soft and low, and she spoke in English. She said: "He followed me—I did as you directed—I had stolen the map from the home of Mustapha the dragoman, and just as I had regained the street, I heard Mustapha talking to his brother who owns the shop below. Had he not stopped to talk, he might have come up and caught me. As it was, I heard him say that the son of Professor Glenhaven and his friends were arriving today—and that he was going to meet them at the Savoy Hotel. So, I trailed him, watched him contact them, then followed them back to Mustapha's home. They went upstairs but came down almost at once. Halfway back to the hotel this fool dropped out and hid in a doorway. I think he thought I didn't see him, but I was aware all the time that he was trailing me, in turn.

"I watched the party go into their hotel, then I made my way here, knowing this fool was following me. I came in, warned you, and you did the rest, of course... Now that we have one of them, shall we kill him?" The callousness of the tone of voice she spoke in shook me a little. Life apparently, in her eyes, was very cheap!

The other was a man. His voice sounded, I judged, like that of a cultured man. Somehow he impressed me as being a foreigner, even though there was no accent to his words, and they were spoken in faultless English.

"No—we do not wish to stir up a hornet's nest unless it is absolutely necessary! No, we shall not kill him. I will speak to him, and then..." The torch advanced a few feet nearer. The man addressed me: "I take it you are a member of the Glenhaven party, and that you have come to continue excavations of the Tomb of Ko Len Tep?"

"You can take it any way you wish!" I rapped, not feeling in any mood for discussing private affairs with him. He chuckled—a soft, loathsome chuckle, which ran up my spine chillingly.

"Of course, there is no need for you to answer. It is quite obvious that you are a member of the party. But I wish you to understand this, and to convey it to your friends: There is much danger for you at the tomb. Indeed, you will never get that far—none of you! You have now lost the map, but knowing Mustapha as I do, I have no doubt he will be able to guide you to the spot.

"This we may prevent, but even if he did guide you, you would meet nothing but death there—far out in the wastes of the desert, where the vultures would pick on your rotting, sun-bleached carcass; where no caravan ever passes, for the tomb is in an out-of-the-way spot, far from the caravan routes.

"I am warning you now, and I desire you to warn all your friends. Forget about the diggings and go your ways in peace. Or remember them, and—go your way to death!"

92

"Rot," I said, as calmly as I could. "You sound like the last act of a lousy melodrama!"

"Perhaps you will think differently, shortly. Hold the torch my dear, while I convince our heroic friend that we are not joking!"

The torch beam danced and wavered as it was passed to the woman, then, holding it low on my helpless figure, she came forward to within about two feet of me. Into the radius of the beam stepped a pair of male legs, wearing dark blue serge trousers. They paused by my side, and the rest of the body was hidden in the darkness above me. I heard a belt being unbuckled, and the man said:

"Rather a childish method of effecting punishment—but at the same time, a very effective one! There is a heavy buckle on this belt, and I fear it may strike you in the face. So, if you will be good enough to roll on to your side, it will help. You see, this is merely a warning, and I have no wish to actually ruin your eyes..."

I knew I was in for it! There was no mercy, no mirth in the words the man spoke. They were deadly serious. He meant that about my eyes! And I obeyed. I rolled over as far as I could, until my features were pressed against the wall.

The belt was raised—I could hear it swishing through the air. Then it smashed with head-numbing force, against the back of my neck. A gasp of pain escaped me as the heavy buckle cut into the soft flesh, and I could feel the warm blood trickling down below my crumpled collar. Again it fell, this time striking me a blow on the crown of my head—a blow which caused every tooth in my skull to shriek protestingly in their nerves. This time I could not repress a cry of sheer pain, and the belt fell again, deflecting against the wall, curling over and into my face, smashing home in my open lips!

I tasted salt blood, and heard the man's voice:

"I'm afraid you'll have to try to get closer to the wall if you wish to save your eyes!" In a daze of agony, I tried to comply with this warning.

How many times the belt fell after that I can't recall. It could have been a hundred times or more, and after a while the world was just a torture-filled globe, in which my racked body screamed out for release from its agony.

And finally, through the weird mistiness which floated before my eyes, the wall became visible again, and I realised that the thrashing—if such a word could adequately describe the ordeal—was over.

"I have finished with you for the moment," said the man, his tone unmoved, "but please remember that this is nothing compared to the miseries you will suffer if you persist in your futile endeavours to open the Tomb of Ko Len Tep! Please warn your companions of that, also—perhaps, when they see the state you are in, they will think twice about going further with their plans!

"I am afraid I shall have to knock you unconscious once more, but I will make it swift and sure this time. When you come round your bonds will have been removed, and you will be free to return to your party. We shall be gone, and it will do you no good to have this house investigated! It has been untenanted for years, and we use it only occasionally as a meeting place. After this we shall use it no more!"

I opened my mouth to speak, to ask how I could get back to the hotel, or something like that. But before my voice could frame the question, the torch beam clicked out, there was a step immediately beside me, and a heavy object smashed down on the back of my neck!

The darkness became shot with a thousand coloured lights; pinpoints of fire whirled before me in a mad galaxy, and then my mind was flying through a black void, and my body had ceased to exist, for the time being...

*　　*　　*　　*

Light glimmered faintly on my consciousness, and I forced my sticky, gummed-up eyelids open, and saw that the night had passed, and daylight was streaming through the nearby window.

I had regained consciousness from the last blow while it was still dark, but the ordeal I had suffered had robbed my weary form of vitality; and in spite of excruciating pain which swelled and ebbed in my brain and head, I had fallen into a sleep of exhaustion.

And now it was morning—or was it afternoon? As the man had promised, my hands were free. Licking my dry lips and working my parched tongue about my raw mouth to induce the salivary glands to moisten it, I stumbled from the place. I came on to the road again, found it was quite early morning, with few people about. I wiped some of the blood from me with a handkerchief and commenced to stagger along in search of aid.

CHAPTER 4

THE PARTY AT SHEPHEARD'S

How I ever managed to get back to the Savoy without flopping out on the way I don't know. I was fortunate enough to obtain a lift from an early motorist, and I think it was this that saved me from fainting on the way.

But when I did arrive back, my friends were roused immediately, and while a doctor dressed my wounds, I informed them of my ordeal. When I was through, they both looked extremely serious, and Ron said: "We didn't quite know what to do when you didn't come back last night. We thought of getting in touch with the police but decided to give you until this morning to return. For all we knew, you might have met some lady friend—you always were a fairly weak character where the ladies were concerned, you must admit!"

I smiled painfully. I knew he was referring to one or two episodes which had taken place while I was still at Oxford—and which, if they had seen the light of publicity, would undoubtedly have resulted in my being 'sacked' from there immediately. I remember there was a girl in the local public-house we patronized, who...but that's quite irrelevant to this story, so I won't bother you with it.

"But," went on Ron, "now we've heard your story I think we'd better contact the police immediately! Did you say you had noted the address of the place to which you were taken?"

"I did—but I'm afraid it won't be any use the police searching there—the fellow told me they wouldn't be using the house again, and it had been empty for years."

"Can't lose anything by trying," said Ron, and he took a note of the address and hurried away to the phone.

The next hour or so was very trying. While I stacked away a healthy breakfast, proving thereby that the thrashing I had taken hadn't had much lasting effect, except on my appearance, I was fussed over by the major and minor members of the Egyptian gendarmerie. They took copious notes, they examined each injury I had sustained, and acted for all the world like a bunch of old hens about to give birth.

Finally, they departed, hurling back expressions of regret that such a terrible thing should have happened to an honoured visitor, and promising that fearful vengeance would be visited upon the heads of my assailants—if they could be found.

When they had gone, we speculated much on the probabilities of what had happened, and Alan said we mustn't forget to warn Mustapha of what the man had threatened. Possibly, in view of the threat to his life, our faithful dragoman would not be so keen on accompanying us!

But he was undeterred when we told him, and just as game as ever for the expedition. He did, however, make us a brief map of the exact location of the tomb, as near as he could recall it, saying smilingly that this was in case the gentleman carried out his threat.

Ron took charge of this, and then I retired for a rest. I woke up just as evening shadows were falling, and found Ron in my room, talking in low tones with Alan. When they saw I was with them again, Ron said: "How're you feeling, Tony?"

I tested my head cautiously with a slight nudge of the hand. Apart from a dull throb there seemed little the matter with it. "Not so bad," I smiled, "but I must look a fearful fright with all this sticking plaster on me!"

"You do look rather like Wells' *Invisible Man*," assented Alan.

"We almost woke you up," Ron told me. "In fact, that's what we were arguing about when you opened your eyes. You see, Alan here has received an invitation from an old friend of his father's, who says he would like him and his friends to join him at Shepheard's Hotel at nine, where he is throwing a late dinner party especially for us. Alan said we ought to let you sleep, but I rather thought you'd like to come—in spite of the plaster! You usually like to be in on anything that's going on, and if you'd awakened and found we'd gone out without you, I expect you would have been crusty about it!"

"I certainly would—I'd have been fuming! I'm not so bad that I'm not fit to attend a quiet dinner party, I hope. Who's the host?"

"Guy called Solidan," explained Alan. "His firm used to handle all the shipping for my father, and since he runs the concern over here, the old guv'nor used to see quite a lot of him. Actually, he's one of the partners in the firm of Fortham and Selidan, but not a very important partner. His brother and his uncle own the firm, and it seems old Selidan is the proverbial poor relation, and since they needed someone to run the Egyptian offices, this Arnold Selidan was their man. He's a fascinating chap, and what he doesn't know about Egypt isn't worth knowing. I once met him when he was on leave in England—he came to dinner at Glenhaven Towers. I suppose he feels he owes me a dinner over here in repayment."

"Then count me in," I told them. "I fail to see why you two should have all the fun!"

"I know just what's in that odious mind of yours," grinned Alan, "but I rather fancy you'll be wrong—I'm afraid there won't be very many ladies present. Only Selidan and his wife, I should think. He married a charming English girl on his last leave and brought her back to roost with him!"

"To roost? Really Alan, at times you're positively indelicate!" grinned Ron.

They helped me to change and made me look as presentable as possible. About an hour or so later we took a taxi to the hotel, mentioned to a waiter that we were members of Mr. Selidan's party, and were escorted to his table. As Alan had predicted, there was no one else besides Selidan and his wife. As we made our salutations, he smilingly introduced us to her.

"Gentlemen, this is my wife Elsa, who, believe me, helps to make life over here endurable for me!"

We graciously acknowledged the introduction to the dark haired, exotic beauty who was Elsa Selidan. Had I not been told by Alan that the girl was English, I should have set her down as Oriental, possibly even a pure Arab strain. She was that type of girl: there was none of the conventional English 'rose' in her. Her skin was dark, almost swarthy, and her eyes were darker yet. Her hair was dressed in an unaffected style, and fell in raven black ringlets upon her shoulders, soft and brown. Her dress was of a type which combines the essence of simplicity with the height of sophistication—no, perhaps that is too ambiguous. Instead, I will say that the dress, although simply cut, was yet more stylish than the latest Parisienne gown could have been. It revealed the tops of her firm, brown, swelling breasts, and the shady hollow between them. When she rose, it fell about her full hips like a skin, and when she sat it outlined the glorious curves of her legs. Had I been a villain in a mid-Victorian play, I should most certainly have smacked my lips at the sight of Elsa Selidan.

Dinner passed off with Selidan talking most of the time, and we found him a most amusing and instructive talker. His wife spoke only when he addressed her, and then merely to agree with the things he said, or to recall some date or incident to his mind. She was a silent, rather mysterious woman, given to staring broodingly at nothing in particular, but always ready to answer when she was addressed. This, more than anything else, seemed to make it less believable than ever that she was English.

It was only after the meal was completed and Selidan had suggested we should all retire to his rooms for a liqueur and a smoke, that he broached the subject of my sticking plasters. I had noticed that he had glanced at me curiously during the meal, and wondered whether his natural curiosity would overcome his English dislike of intruding upon the personal affairs of his guests. But when we were comfortably settled, he said: "Pardon my curiosity, Mr. Gilmour, but you appear to have met with a misfortune of some description? I trust it did not occur here, in Cairo?"

"I'm afraid it did, Mr. Selidan," I told him, and seeing no reason why he should not hear the story, I told him all. When I had finished, he tapped his cigar thoughtfully on an ashtray, and gazed at me from his pale blue eyes. He ran his hand through his corn-coloured hair, and his fresh complexioned features registered sympathy.

"It is an outrage," he said, at length. "Have the police done anything in the matter?"

"I believe they have investigated the empty house—and found it to be merely an empty house and nothing more. They were most solicitous when they called, but since then they seem to have reached the conclusion that it was my own fault for prowling about the city unescorted."

"Disgusting!" snapped Selidan. "I shall see if I cannot put in a word or two to make them move a little quicker! I am not without some influence over here."

"Please don't bother," I told him. "I'm afraid they will not be able to find out anything worthwhile. You see, I was unable to give a description of the persons—I never saw them. Added to which I have the feeling they tried to disguise their voices."

"Oh, I see. Yes, in that case it must be rather awkward for the authorities to find them. But what could be the purpose at the back of such an attack?"

Alan cut in here, his face serious. "You remember how his father was killed?" he asked, and Selidan nodded, a regretful expression flickering over his face. "Well," said Alan, "we're over here to find out why he was killed!"

"Why he was killed? But—but I had assumed that the death was accidental? That is what we were given to understand!"

"We think differently, Mr. Selidan. We think there is some deep mystery attached to this Egyptian Tomb, and we applied for a permit to continue excavations. It would have been easy enough for whoever is interested in the matter to find out that we had obtained the permit and intended to resume the exploration of the Tomb. And we also think that whoever is making the mistake of assuming that we can be frightened off, is butting his head against not a stone wall, but a wall of steel! Isn't that so?"

We nodded, and Selidan poured fresh drinks. He said: "So you are determined to continue? I admire your courage gentlemen! Possibly there is much ground for your suspicions; this country has many bigger mysteries than even the Sphinx. And possibly you have stumbled upon one of these mysteries. But be careful, I beg you! Sometimes these mysteries have been preserved by the sacrifice of life! The men behind them will stop at nothing and will count murder a minor matter where their personal well-being is at stake. We have known such men, and have seen them finally brought to justice, but not before severe harm had been done to those who finally rounded them up. Is that not so, my dear?"

"It is, Arnold," agreed his wife, in her husky tones.

"I personally shall speak to the head of the police department," continued Selidan. "I will ensure that you receive all the help you may need while you are here. Once you are out in the desert it is another matter, of course!"

"Thank you, but I don't anticipate any further trouble here," smiled Alan.

"I don't know," Selidan mused. "If the persons who wish to prevent you opening the Tomb are as desperate as you tell me, they will take every opportunity to do you injury. Much of the East is incomprehensible to you but I have lived here most of my days and understand much which you would not. Should you run into anything further, be sure of my help. It will be given willingly, and the influence I hold with the authorities would persuade them to investigate much more closely than if you were to approach them. I beg of you, count me as an ally."

"We will," said Alan, rising with a smile and taking Selidan's hand, "but now we must be going, Mr. Selidan. It's been a very pleasant evening, and we've thoroughly enjoyed it. I should like to ask you to dine with us, but as we leave tomorrow, I'm afraid it's impossible."

"Perhaps when you return," suggested Selidan, pleasantly. "And in the meantime, take good care of yourselves—and remember to communicate with me should the need arise!"

We promised and took our leave of Selidan and his charming wife. It being a fine, clear night, with a luminous, disc-like moon floating above amid a million stars, we decided to walk back to the hotel. My head had begun to ache abominably, but I kept this to myself, for if my friends had known they might have expected me to consent to the start of our expedition being postponed for a few days, and I did not wish this.

"A decent guy," ruminated Alan, as we walked along, "and I wouldn't be a bit surprised if we did need his help later on."

Ron and I were silent, busy with our thoughts. We reached the hotel, and as we were making our way up to our rooms, one of the messenger boys hurried over and saluted. "A package was delivered, addressed to you three gentlemen," he said. "I placed it in your room, sir!"

"My room?" said Ron, blankly, "a package?"

"Yes sir. It was delivered by an Arab beggar who I did not know."

"Damned funny," mused Ron, "who'd want to deliver packages to us?"

"And who the devil can have sent it?" demanded Ron.

102

"Perhaps we could find out if we went up and had a look into it," I ventured, sarcastically. Ron grinned, and we proceeded upstairs to his room.

The page had placed the parcel on the table. It was quite a large affair, wrapped in strong brown paper, and bearing three names in a scrawling hand. Our three names!

Ron took the bull by the horns, tore off the top layer of paper. Beneath it was yet another. This also he removed, only to come to three layers of stout cardboard. Beneath these was a further layer of paper, and we were beginning to think the whole thing was a silly prank, when he unearthed a small cigarette tin.

He looked at us, and we nodded. He flipped open the lid and we stared down, mesmerised, at the contents. All we could see was a small, ragged lump of red flesh swimming in a pool of rich, red blood.

"What the hell's this?" stammered Ron, gazing at it with startled eyes.

I took a step forward and peered more closely at the object. It was rounded on three sides, but the fourth was raw and bleeding. It looked like a lump of flesh torn forcibly from some portion of the human body. And suddenly I knew what it was with a kind of sick horror. I felt my stomach turn, and I said:

"It's a tongue—a human tongue!"

We stood there staring. And as we stared, a knock came to the door. Ron called:

"Come in!"

One of the police officials we had seen that morning entered. He looked very grave and failed to see what Ron held in the tin. He said: "You gentlemen had a native guide named Mustapha...?"

"Why, yes," said Ron, hardly hearing the question, for his bewildered attention was still concentrated on the tongue.

103

"I thought I had better tell you," said the official, "that your guide was found murdered at his home this evening. He had been dead for some time, and his death was due to a poisoned dart. The strange thing is that his tongue had been removed!"

CHAPTER 5

TWO HUNDRED MILES DOWN THE NILE

There was no question of it: the tongue which Ron held in that little tin box was undoubtedly poor Mustapha's. The police official agreed that it was and proceeded to explain to us how Mustapha had been discovered in his ramshackle room, poisoned by a tiny blowpipe dart, and with his tongue torn forcibly from its moorings, probably by means of a pair of pincers which were also discovered.

We did all we could to help the investigation, but the police seemed unable to even arrive at any guess as to the identity of the assailants. We told them about the Tomb of Ko Len Tep, and how someone was trying to prevent the diggings going ahead, and the official looked very serious and said he would report the matter to his chief.

Ron and myself went to headquarters, and after being assured that we could not help in any way and that we must now leave the law to take its course, we applied for permission to continue our expedition, which was granted without any fuss.

As we returned to our hotel, a gaudily robed, bearded dragoman detached himself from the crowd of beggars, thieves and idlers, and deferentially approached us. "Good morning, sairs," he exclaimed in broken English, "my name is Mahmud—I am the second brother of that poor one who be lying dead, Mustapha."

"I see, Mahmud; we are very, very sorry."

"Thank you, sair. But I be here to ask you a thing."

"Then ask on by all means. If it's about the poor chap being buried…"

"Oh no, sair! That be of no matter. The police will attend to that. It be about Mustapha's—what you say?—wheel!"

"Wheel?" echoed Ron and I, surprised.

"Yes, sairs, wheel! You know—how it is, he leaves to me as his only brother all which he owns."

"I see now, you mean—will!"

"That be so, sair."

"You want the money we owe him for organizing our little expedition?"

"Not that, sair. You see, Mustapha, he now being no more, you will be needing someone who to take his position. Now I be one good dragoman, also, and since he also leave me everything else, he leave me you as much."

"Oh! He left you us, did he? So, you want to apply for his job?"

"That be it, sair."

"You know the country pretty well?"

"So well like the bottom of my foot, sair. Me be best dragoman in all the world! You hire me?"

Ron glanced at me, and I said: "Up to Alan, really, but since this poor chap's lost his brother, I don't see why we shouldn't give him the job."

"I gather the impression he isn't much worried about his brother," smiled Ron. "What he seems to be thinking of is how much he can make out of his brother's death! Very well, Mahmud, subject to Mr. Glenhaven's approval, you can consider yourself hired as of today. I suppose Mustapha gave you some idea of this trip?"

"He do not tell so much, sair. But I find out what is this!"

"Well, I understand he has two strong trucks, all supplies, and a half-dozen native workmen waiting for us down at Asyut. We start today on the Nile steamer—there will be four in the party which goes down to Asyut—Mr. Glenhaven, Mr. Gilmour, myself and you. The boat leaves in an hour, so if you will be good enough to superintend the removal of our personal luggage, we will join you down at the boat."

106

The man's swarthy, bearded face burst into a wide smile. He said, gleefully: "Very good, sair! I go about your business now, quicko!" He vanished from sight, his dark hair mingling with the crowd.

"Thank Heaven for that," said Ron. "I thought we'd have to start mooching about for another dragoman, but we're in luck!"

We went into the hotel and completed our arrangements for leaving. Within an hour we were all safely embarked on the household flat-iron shaped steamboat, jostling amidst a throng of eager tourists.

"This is a slow way," Ron explained, "but if you want to see something of the country; it's the best way. The boat stops at various show places, and you'll get the chance of seeing the pyramids. Mind you, you'll have to go on the conducted tour! There's a fellow on this boat who acts as guide, and he'll show you around with the rest of the flock."

"How about you doing the honours?" I suggested. "After all, I hardly like the idea of milling about with all these folks! And if we have to ride a donkey to the pyramids and the Tomb of Ti at Saqqara, as the guidebook says, it's six miles, and we're going to cut a sorry picture mounted on donkeys!"

"I'd like to," nodded Ron, "but I'm not very well up in this section of the country. I know Cairo fairly well, but down the Nile I'm as much a stranger as you two are."

But on the whole it wasn't so bad as I had thought it would be. Our guide proved to be an amusing fellow, speaking a weird mixture of classical and broken English, and recounting to us a strange and utterly untrue outline of Egyptian history, which, however, seemed to satisfy the tourists perfectly.

We met some interesting characters: the American, who said he was considering buying the Sphinxes and having it re-erected in his Long Island garden, the Scotsman who grumbled and groused about every piastre he had to fork out, and two dear old maiden ladies who were half afraid that we should be seized upon by bands of roving Bedouins and robbed and killed.

These were the people who sat at our table, and it was most entertaining to listen to their conversation night after night. The American was extremely anxious to reach Karnak—he was obsessed by the idea of Sphinxes and was in a dither to walk down the Avenue of Sphinxes at Karnak. I should, I must admit, have liked to have seen this sight myself, but unfortunately, we should be leaving the boat at Asyut, over a hundred miles from Karnak and Luxor.

And so the days passed pleasantly enough, on conducted tours and in friendly conversation, and at last we were seeing the real Egypt, the Egypt of the Nile Valley between Cairo and the first cataract: the date palms lining the banks, the white-robed camel riders visible in the distance, the mud villages, the natives, the fierce hawk-eyed Arabs astride magnificent Arabian whites, and the unending yellow waters of the fabulous Nile. It was a trip packed with interest to the three of us, and we passed the days in sight-seeing, and the nights in quiet conversation, discussing all we had seen that day.

Mahmud was on the boat, but we did not see him very often: I suppose, being a native, he chose not to mingle with the other passengers—although there were several of the Egyptian well-to-do on board, and these mixed freely and were inclined, if anything, to look down on we tourists. Possibly it was because Mahmud was a servant that he was kept out of the way.

We were rapidly nearing Asyut: It was late at night, and a clear moon shone down from a star-spangled sky. I was taking a stroll about the deck when I came across Alan and Ron, both leaning over the rail, talking in low tones.

"What gives?" I demanded, settling beside them.

"We were talking about the expedition," Ron told me, gazing fixedly at the Nile. "We're getting pretty near Asyut now, and it's been a very pleasant trip. But now we'll have to turn our minds to business. I think we'll have to move very carefully!"

"Look here," said Alan, uneasily, "this really isn't your show, you know. I mean—it wasn't your father who was killed—well, what I mean is, it isn't exactly your affair, and there seems to be some danger..."

"I hope you're not driving at what I think you're driving at, Alan," said Ron.

Alan twiddled uneasily with his coat button. He said:

"I've been thinking it over, and after all that's happened— you know, poor Mustapha, Tony being beaten-up, and that ghastly tongue—it's struck me that I haven't any right to expect you two to rush into danger on my account. I mean to say, if you'd like to carry on to Luxor, well, I'll be able to manage this business myself—I hope."

"You flatter yourself, you chump," grinned Ron. "You don't speak a syllable of the lingo."

"Maybe not, but Mahmud speaks English—or what passes for it! I'd rub along."

"Are you hinting that you don't want us?" asked Ron, with a wink at me.

"Absolutely not!"

"Then what the hell do you mean by inferring that we'd even consider letting you go on your own now?" demanded Ron, wrathfully. "Why, you chump, what was it you bought off that beggar in front of the hotel for three hundred piastres? A dirty bit of rag!"

"Dirty bit of rag nothing," protested Alan. "That was a genuine piece of Cleopatra's winding cloth! The chap swore on the beard of the Prophet!"

"I daresay he did. In fact, it's a wonder he didn't try to sell you the beard of the Prophet, you ass!"

"As a matter of fact," said Alan, rather shamefacedly, "he did."

109

"You're the absolute limit," I laughed. "And then you think you can manage by yourself!"

"I didn't mean it like that," said Alan. "All I meant was I didn't like the idea of dragging you two into danger!"

"We know what you meant, Alan," said Ron, softly, slapping him on the shoulder, "and we appreciate it. But we're in this with you to the end—besides your dad, there's Mustapha gone, and I daresay Tony wants to settle with someone for that beating up he had. Let's make a pact right here: that no matter what happens to any one of us, the other—or others—will carry on to the bitter end!"

We all nodded silently, and in turn gripped each other's hands tightly. Then we drove the thought of unpleasant possibilities from our minds.

CHAPTER 6

KHAN EL SHEMS

Asyut is a strange and interesting place. On our first quick walk through it, I was intrigued by the many bazaars I saw, and enthralled by the wondrous shawls which are made there, and which are distinctive from those made anywhere else in Egypt. Pottery also, made from some fine red clay, was in abundance, and there were many rare pieces I should have liked to have purchased to take home. As it was, I contented myself with buying one of the peculiar, silver-fringed shawls, which Ron said I had been grossly overcharged for, and which Alan skitted would be a help and comfort to me in my old age.

Here, the spoken sound of the Arabic tongue had changed; in certain words the pronunciation seemed altogether different, and I found it increasingly difficult to understand what was being said. Consequently I had to rely on Ron, and he fulfilled the role of interpreter excellently.

We found ourselves, late that evening, standing outside an Arab Inn, bearing a dingy wooden sign, reading: 'Khan El Shems', which Ron explained meant, literally, 'Inn of the Sun'. Mahmud had been absent all day, marshalling our trucks and stores and attending to last minute details for our start on the morrow; and we had a free night before us.

From the interior of the Inn of the Sun came the sibilant flute-like music of the East: the beating of a monotonous tom-tom, the warbling of reed flutes, and mingled with these noises, the chatter and laughter of rough, coarse-speaking Arabs from the villages and hills.

"I've been thinking," said Alan, "how about seeing the night life?"

Ron looked thoughtful and pursed his lips. He said: "I don't know, Alan. We're in a fairly low quarter here. We wouldn't be the first tourists to have our throats cut in Asyut, you know!"

"I bet we'd be the first to put up the fight we would put up, prior to the cutting process," grunted Alan.

"Certainly we ought to visit one of these cafés; they are really a mixture of inn and eating place, you know. And there is generally some entertainment going on."

"Entertainment?" queried Alan. "Fine! But nothing like the half-dressed shows at the Windmill back home, eh?"

"Better—or worse, according to your views on that sort of thing," grinned Ron. "Here they have Arab girls dancing, and their dances are sometimes so primitive as to be embarrassing."

"What are we arguing for?" I snorted. "Let's get in! Hell, we aren't a bunch of kids!"

"All right, we'll take a chance," said Alan, "but keep yourselves to yourselves, and don't make any funny cracks! Remember, it's quite astonishing to know how many Arabs can speak a smattering of English—and understand a good deal more. They—well, most of them—rely on the tourist trade for their living, and therefore it's essential to the majority to be able to make themselves understood in quite a number of languages. They're highly intelligent, and inordinately cunning."

Prepared for almost anything, we entered the inn, and led by Ron, moved over to a small table in a corner. The atmosphere was dull and smoky, so smoky that Alan broke into a spasm of coughing as we sat down. Many glances were cast at us, but none of them openly hostile.

We settled down, after Ron had ordered something, to enjoy the strange surroundings in which we found ourselves. The place was lit by flickering lamps, and the orchestra, composed of three men, squatted cross legged in one corner. Along the back of the inn a long, coloured curtain was drawn,

112

and the lean Arabs, seated around drinking and laughing, kept glancing continually towards this.

A hush fell as the music commenced to wail again, and from behind the curtains, into a small square space in the centre of the floor, appeared the figure of a heavily veiled girl. She was, at the moment, shapeless, owing to the multi-shaded swathings about her, but her movements were graceful, and as she slowly went into a dance, the bangles and ornaments on her slim ankles jangled and clinked. She made no sound; her feet were bare, and very shapely.

The Arabs had ceased to laugh and joke, and were leaning forward, eyes afire with something more than interest, as the girl went into her dance. I found myself leaning forward as eagerly as they, for although the girl's face was as yet concealed from me, a curious, pulse-quickening excitement had gripped me and riveted my attention to that solitary lithe figure, alone amongst these fierce-eyed sons of the sand.

I heard Ron chuckle beside me. He said: "Hmm! You're in luck! Seems you're going to be treated to a session of the Dance of the Seven Veils!"

"I've heard of it," I murmured, still staring at the dancer; "isn't the idea to discard the veils?"

"Exactly. It's just an ancient version of strip tease! There's nothing new."

The veils were commencing to fall to the floor now, but slowly, slowly, one at a time, and still the dance continued.

"Gentlemen shouldn't look at this sort of carry on," said Alan.

"Then why look?" asked Ron.

"I'm not a gentleman," Alan explained, and continued to look.

Four of the veils now lay on the floor, and flashing glimpses of a lithe brown body were visible. Well, not exactly brown, but a shade like that of coffee made with rich cream; a

113

fragrant refreshing colour. My breath came more quickly as the girl danced on, now with only a single veil as covering. Her body was young, strong, firm; her hair dark and neatly arranged. Her face, from the little I could see of it, was small and oval, and tiny white teeth flashed as she smiled and whirled her last veil.

And then the veil had fallen, and before I could realize it, she was gone through the curtains, to the accompaniment of roars of applause, and one or two suggestive shouts. I heard Ron speaking and jerked my thoughts back to him.

"That's funny," he was saying. "I could swear that girl is not the usual type of dancer! I should have said that she was a modern Egyptian girl of pure strain. Look how her hair was coiffured! She's the first Arab girl I've seen with hair done in a modern style; at least, dancing in such a place."

"What makes you think she's different to the usual type?" I asked him.

"Well, nothing I could actually lay a finger on, Tony. But the girls who dance here generally come from the Ouled Naïl Tribes, and wander from place to place, entertaining. And that girl doesn't look like an Almee to me."

He allowed the matter to drop, but I could not tear myself away from my thoughts of that gracious figure, slim and supple, living by entertaining coarse Arabs, by exhibiting her slender form for the pleasure of tribesmen and villagers.

I was still staring towards the curtain at the back of the Inn when I could have sworn I saw it open a little, and a pair of dark inquisitive eyes peered through. I nudged Ron, and drew his attention to this, but by the time he had turned to look they were gone again.

"A pair of eyes," I told him. "I couldn't be sure, but they might have been the eyes of that dancing girl!"

Ron smiled: "You're dreaming!"

I relapsed into silence, but kept my eyes fixed upon that dark curtain. And sure enough, the eyes were there again! But this time there was a hand, also! A slim, beckoning hand! The eyes stared into mine, and the hand indicated the exit.

I felt my breath coming faster, and I glanced at Ron and Alan to see if they had noticed. Then I said, lightly: "I think I'll shove along outside for a breath of air!"

Ron smiled and rose. He said: We're about ready to go ourselves, aren't we, Alan?"

"Okay by me."

"No—don't bother, I don't want to drag you two out of here."

"No bother at all," said Ron. "Best for us all to hang together—or we'll probably hang separately,"

"Well, to tell you the truth, I'm going to see a lady! Someone beckoned to me from behind that curtain—beckoned to me to go outside... I think it was the dancer!"

"Delirious," said Alan, sympathetically. "He's been standing in the sun on that Nile steamer too long, Ron!"

"You idiot! I tell you—"

"Yes, we know all about it," said Ron, soothingly, "but what you want to do is to go home to bed! Remember what happened the last time you ran after a lady in Cairo!"

This sobered me for a second. Then I said: "But this is different, I tell you! She did beckon me!"

Alan glanced at Ron, and Ron back at Alan. Then with common accord, they took an arm each and escorted me, futilely protesting, outside the Inn of the Sun. "Let go, you fools," I grunted, trying to shake them off. But they merely grinned and hung on tighter.

"This is terrible," said Alan. "Just like that time at Oxford when we had to forcibly restrain him from eloping with the barmaid!"

"You fools," I panted, "I hadn't any sense then..."

115

"That's why we're looking after you now," grinned Ron. "If, as you say, the lady wants to see you, well, let her come! Let 'em all come, in fact. Perhaps there'll be one for Alan and me as well!"

"You don't understand—I could tell by the way she looked at me that she wanted to see me alone!"

"I suppose she did! And then she'd waft you away to some Egyptian clip-joint, and you'd most likely get your throat slit!"

"But...she may have wanted to tell me something!"

"She probably did! About how she's supporting her old mother, and is usually a good girl, but...they're all the same the world over, women!"

"Will you let go and clear off, you pair of idiots?"

"Not on your life, Tony Gilmour! You're not going to have anything to do with any dusky adventuresses, or any other kind of esses as long as we're here. Yank him along, Alan!" And so, they dragged me, still protesting, away from the neighbourhood.

On thinking it over, back at the shabby little hotel, I agreed with them that it had been a good thing for me they had done so. Probably, as Ron had said, the girl was just after "baksheesh," and I would have had a nasty time of it if she had had a number of Arab friends about to knock me silly and rob me.

We ate a little, then sat smoking and talking over the things to be done before the expedition started tomorrow. Mahmud rolled up, bowed profoundly, and informed us that all was in order, and that the trucks were ready, and also the equipment and workmen. But during our conversation, I couldn't help thinking of the girl who had danced the Dance of the Seven Veils, and of what she had wanted me for when she had beckoned from behind that curtain.

Perhaps the signal hadn't been intended for me at all: perhaps there was some bold, bad Sheik present who had captivated her heart, and it had been to him she was motioning.

But no! That signal had been definitely meant for me! Hadn't she looked straight into my eyes when she had given it?

Ron and Alan noticed I was preoccupied, and I suppose they guessed where my thoughts were running. They didn't attempt to draw me out, though, and shortly after Mahmud had gone, Ron rose, stretched his arms, yawned, and said: "I'll turn in, I think. Got a busy day ahead tomorrow!"

Alan joined him, and they both said goodnight, and went along to their rooms. I sat on for a time longer, then followed.

Our rooms were on the ground floor, and it had been evident when we had arrived that morning that they were no miracles of purity and sanitation. Fly specks formed a tasteful decoration on the otherwise bare walls, and fleas were hopping about the floor gaily, quite visible, and seemingly prepared to strike up an eating acquaintanceship with whoever was to occupy the room. I hoped they would not like my taste!

I decided not to take off my drill trousers, so I simply slid out of the thin jacket I was wearing over an equally thin singlet. There was no light in the room, so I threw myself immediately on to the bed in the corner, feeling too hot to bother with the dirty sheets which covered it. And as I landed on it, a tiny gasp came from under me, and I felt the squirming of human flesh against my body!

CHAPTER 7

THE DANCING GIRL OF ASYUT

I don't suppose I lay there for more than a second, then I jumped high in the air and landed on my back on the hard, flea-ridden floor. I mean, there are two schools of thought on this bed business: I could tell by the gasp I heard that the figure in mine was a lady—probably a young lady! I'm not denying that some chaps, in a situation like this, would have leaped to the fray with glad cries; they'd have looked on the matter as a Heaven-sent opportunity. But I'm different: I mean, not so much different, but in spite of my liking for the fair sex, I usually like to be introduced to the members of it whom I am going to find in my bed. Besides which, I also am very keen on knowing just what they are doing in my bed—if they have a knife, if they have mistaken the room, or if they are merely feeling lonely!

So I got up hastily, and was in time to witness the shape of a woman rising from the bed and stepping out into the rays of the moon which came through the window. The Seven Veils Dancer of the Inn of the Sun!

I had only glimpsed her features previously, but it had been an unforgettable glimpse! Now I saw them clearly in the moonbeams, clear and close, and I was thrilled as I have never been before or since. Eastern or not, the girl had more charm than a barrow-load of Hollywood glamour girls, a shapelier figure than any mannequin in London, Paris or New York; and a pair of deep, dark eyes which would have made the Mona Lisa tear her hair in green envy!

And I was sure she was no dancing girl; she couldn't have been. Her fingers, visible in the moonbeams, were manicured about the nails, and were soft and supple as if they had had the best of care and attention. Her lips were slightly parted, and to one side I could dimly see—a gold tooth!

She was perhaps twenty-one or two. I am no judge of a girl's years.

I stammered, sounding, I admit, like the chorus of a Carmen Miranda song.

She smiled a perfect smile and said: "You are shocked, perhaps? You wish to know what the devil I am doing in your room? You desire to know who I am?"

"And—er—if you intend to remain," I put in.

She regarded me from eyes which were now veiled by her long sweeping lashes. She arranged her robes a little, decorously, and a half smile played over her face. In that moment I forgot how I had found her, what she was up to when I had entered, or why she had come. I could think only of the moonlight playing on her dark hair, of her mysterious eyes which looked full into mine, of the way her garments lined the youthful curves of her body.

Had she had a knife handy, she might have plunged it into my heart before I would have awakened from my contemplation of her dark beauty.

But finally she said: "I am here to warn you. I tried to get in touch with you tonight at the inn—but when your friends took you away, I was afraid to follow immediately. You see, I must be so careful!" Her English was perfect, without accent. Her voice was vibrant and compelling. "I risked much to come here and see you—and you must ask me nothing as to who or what I am. Just know me for now as the Dancing Girl of Asyut!"

"I'm afraid I don't understand you—you came to warn me, you say? About what?"

She made an impatient gesture. "You must know that! Did you not have trouble in Cairo? And if you continue with your plans, you will have more trouble. You may even be killed!"

119

I threw the magic of her presence away from me, stepped forward and gripped her roughly by a smooth, supple arm. I growled: "Is this another trick? Who sent you here?"

"It is no trick, I swear. No one sent me here. I came of my own free will, because I would not like to see three Englishmen be murdered."

"But you know about us? Too much! How can a dancing girl know about what happened to us in Cairo? How can a dancing girl speak such good English? Tell me—were you the woman who trapped me into following her, back in Cairo? Were you?"

I had tightened my grip on her arm, and she winced. She said: "Had I been that woman, should I be here now, warning you?"

"You could be! It might be some trick to try to persuade us not to carry out the excavations!"

"I am not what I seem," she said. "Please believe that. I am thinking only of what is best for all of us!"

"Nonsense! How could you be anything but what you seem? Who else but a common dancing girl would expose herself in such a way before the lewd eyes of those damned Arabs? And yet, what kind of dancing girl are you?"

"I am a mystery, Mr. Gilmour. Let's leave it at that!"

"You know my name?"

"I do! And I had thought you were a gentleman. But your low remark about my dancing tonight has exposed you for nothing but a boor! You see only superficialities—you should look deeper!"

"I'm sorry for that remark," I said, genuinely contrite, "but I thought you were tricking me in some way. I have always been susceptible to beautiful women, and my boorishness was more a method of self-protection than a desire to be crude and vulgar."

"I accept that explanation. And now, will you accept my warning? Will you?"

"I am sorry again, but it is impossible. We are sworn, my friends and I, to complete this expedition."

"You still doubt my good faith?"

"Even if I believed implicitly, my answer would have to be the same. The matter does not rest with me alone!"

She was silent, and she drew nearer. Her eyes gazed up into mine, and there was a sudden, wonderful magic in the moonlight which fell across her face in bars of light and bars of darkness where the rods of the Venetian blinds cut across it. "I know your kind," she said. "Isn't there a song in your country about mad dogs and Englishmen going out in the noonday sun? Well, you will be going out in more than that if you journey to the Tomb of Ko Len Tep!"

"Nevertheless, we shall go," I told her, unmoved.

"Then God go with you," she whispered, and leaning upwards, her lips brushed mine swiftly.

Before I had recovered from the shock, she had thrust the blind aside, and had vanished into the shadows of the date palms which surrounded the hotel. And the roses in that Egyptian hotel garden seemed to cast back her fleeting fragrance...

CHAPTER 8

INTO THE DESERT

We assembled at the starting point the following morning; I hadn't mentioned the incident of the dancing girl's late visit to my friends, for I was uncertain of how they would have taken the news, and I knew well enough that it wouldn't have made the least difference to our arrangements.

Mahmud was waiting for us near the two strong trucks which were to carry us, and with him were some half dozen native workmen—strong, ugly looking fellows, who could toil under the blazing African sun without feeling undue strain.

On my way to the starting point, I saw the dancing girl once again; she was standing in a shop doorway, and, although her face was veiled, I was sure it was she. She was speaking very rapidly to an unkempt, ragged individual who had apparently never heard of such a thing as a razor. He bore in his hand a long wooden staff, and when I caught sight of his eyes, I experienced a shock, for they seemed blank and staring, as if he were blind. About his features were terrible ulcerated places, and his skin was thick and horny, as if some disease had fastened its invidious talons upon his old person. As we passed, he stepped from the doorway and began to hobble rapidly down the road, the passers-by giving him not only wide berths, but looks of disgust and loathing.

Ron caught the direction of my gaze, and a look of pity crossed his face as he saw the old man. "Leprosy," he said briefly. "Quite prevalent hereabouts. They say it's caused by eating rotten fish—the salt tax is so high that properly cured fish is difficult to obtain, you see. I dare say that the authorities will get hold of the poor chap sooner or later and pack him away to some colony."

"I should have thought they'd have done so already."

122

"Not necessarily. It's a common belief that leprosy is highly contagious, but it isn't. I understand that the Sisters of Tracadie have nursed lepers for generations without one contracting the disease. Of course, it is possible to contract it, and since there isn't any known cure for it, practically every nation is agreed that its lepers should be outlawed from the rest of civilisation."

I nodded, amazed again at Ron's erudition. Then the entire matter was driven out of my head as we began to prepare for our start. It was arranged that Ron should drive the foremost truck with Mahmud to guide him and the plan to refer to between them. They would also carry the six native workers and the water supply and food.

Alan and myself were to share the second truck with me driving, and the rest of the excavating equipment in the back, and also two ten-gallon drums of petrol in case the specially large tanks on the trucks failed to see us there and back.

Before we climbed into our places, Ron came quietly up to us and handed us each a revolver and spare cartridges. "Just in case," he smiled. "But let's hope we won't need them!"

And then he had swung back into the front truck, and, under the staring, curious eyes of the tattered little Arab children, we started the trucks into roaring life and moved off majestically into the desert, heading for Farafra Oasis, from which, Mahmud told us, it would be easier to pick up our bearings for the tomb.

Even in a modern, specially constructed truck it's hard going across the desert sands; and it was almost an hour before we had lost sight of the Nile and its surroundings. But finally, we were out in a vast waste of sand stretching as far as the eye could see, and further; illimitable, eternal, always shifting, but always looking the same.

I found out for the first time that the desert is very far from being the flat expanse some people believe it to be. It is never flat; it lifts and falls in undulating ridges and drifts, some so

123

high that once Ron's truck had plunged over them, and down the other side we could no longer see it until we, too, had breasted the dune. It is hard on the eyes, and after gazing at the unbroken goldenness of it for hours they begin to smart and even to water. However, I clung close behind Ron's truck until we called a halt to eat and drink.

The sun was high above us now, blazing relentlessly down from a light-blue sky, and bead of perspiration stood out on our faces as we gulped down drafts of cool, pure water.

Roughly speaking, Ron told us, we had a matter of two hundred and fifty miles to cover to reach the oasis, which was our first stopping point. Here we would rest for the night and refill our water containers. We had now been on the move for a number of hours and had to rely on Mahmud and a small compass for our guidance—and Mahmud informed us that we should, by his reckoning, reach the oasis just before nightfall.

It was with deep feelings of thankfulness that we did reach it eventually; and we tumbled from the trucks stiff and sore, our shoes filled with sand, in spite of the fact that we had been mainly riding. We had brought along tents, and these we pitched for the night under the cool shade of a clump of palms. The natives scorned any such commodities and threw themselves down heedlessly into the sand.

It was a tranquil night, except for one thing: sand fleas. I questioned Ron about these, saying that I was surprised we should find anything living in such a waste of sand. But he reminded me that wandering Arab tribes quite often pitched camp here; and wherever there was, or had been, an Arab encampment, there also would be battalions of fleas.

At the moment, the tents of goatskin belonging to a tribe of wandering Bedouins were pitched not far from our location; and I had an interesting glimpse of the lives of these people. The women were busy about domestic tasks, grinding corn or mixing the evening meal; the men lay sprawled about, or rubbed down their fine horses and watered and fed their camels.

I turned in at last when the swift, rushing darkness of the desert had claimed the Oasis. I was dog-tired, and in spite of a reasonable fear that I should be eaten alive by fleas before the sun rose again, I slept soundly.

I was awakened early; the sun had not yet risen, and I felt I could have slept another half day at least.

"But we have to push on," explained Ron. "About sixty-five miles will see us at the sight of the excavation and we want to cover most of it before that damned sun comes up!"

Wearily I climbed into the driving seat again and Alan shed the gorgeous suit of orange and green pyjamas he had brought along and climbed up beside me.

And so we started out into the desert, coming rapidly nearer to the Tomb of Ko Len Top and the solution of the mystery which surrounded it.

We had covered perhaps forty miles of the route, when, just above the horizon, we suddenly saw a murky greyness hovering. It looked like a cloud to us, and we thought no more of it until Alan suddenly noticed that it was rapidly approaching us. At the same instant, the leading truck stopped and Ron hopped out and ran back to meet us.

"Sandstorm," he gasped. "Cut your engine and stick in your truck! It's constructed to protect you from almost anything and the only danger is that it might overturn. But Mahmud doesn't seem to think so, for he says it doesn't seem to be a very big storm. Whatever you do, don't move from where you are, or you'll get lost in the storm and lose touch altogether with us."

As he raced back towards his own truck, we fastened all the windows in ours and sat tight, waiting for the storm to strike us. There was a rushing noise, and from the west two mighty columns of whirling sand bore down upon us. It was, indeed, a terrifying sight to anyone unaccustomed to it, and, in spite of

125

the much-vaunted invulnerability of our trucks, the fine golden sand penetrated and covered us with a gritty layer of particles.

The desert outside was as grey as a London fog, and everything within a few feet radius was cut off from view entirely.

The storm raged, with our trucks as its centre, for perhaps an hour; and when it had finally died down, we heaved a sigh of relief. We clambered stiffly from the truck and inspected the engine and interior. We were pleased to find that the engine jackets had done their work better than the windows, although the interior of the truck and its contents were almost entirely covered with sand. The wheels were deep in, and to restart the truck it was necessary to fork out some sand mats—coarse sacking with wooden rails roped across it—to restart the truck and get it out of the loose stuff. When this was finally accomplished, we glanced about for the truck containing Ron and Mahmud.

"Hmm!" said Alan. "Could have sworn it was about fifty feet away when that storm hit us!"

"So could I," I agreed. "Perhaps it's over the next ridge, or possibly the storm has raised a ridge in front of us!"

We crossed the wadi and climbed the opposite ridge. It was quite high, some two hundred feet, and when we had reached the summit we were both winded. And we were in for a bad shock, for all we could see were the unbroken ridges of sand running far into the distance.

Of the first truck there was no sign!

CHAPTER 9

SHIPWRECKED ON DRY SAND

We searched like a couple of men possessed; we climbed up and down ridges, ran along wadis, shouted out until our throats were dry and hoarse. But although our shouts carried far in the thin, pure air of the desert, we received no answer. The first truck had apparently vanished into space, leaving not a sign or trace of where it had stood!

And for the first time the seriousness of our position was brought home to us.

We located our truck with some difficulty and took draughts at our water supply. Then we sat down to think things over.

"Damned annoying," said Alan with his usual understatement. "Damnation! Here we are, shipwrecked in the desert!"

"Well, it isn't any use moaning about it," I told him. "The best thing we can do is to decide what to do next."

"That's logical," he admitted. "What do you propose?"

"We've still got our truck. I suggest we trek back to the Oasis. When Ron finds we're lost I fancy he'll go back there for us."

"How do we get back?"

"Simple. Just follow the marks of the truck wheels!"

"Easier said than done. The storm will have washed all trace of those out!"

I bit my lip. I said:

"I think I know the compass course. Let's have your compass, Alan, and we'll work by that."

Alan shrugged apologetically.

"Sorry, but I haven't got one!"

"What!" I howled. "You set off on a three-hundred-mile journey into the blessed trackless desert without supplying yourself with a compass?"

"All right, Tony, we'll use yours!"

I coughed a little. "Hem! I rather fancy I forgot, too. I had quite a lot on my mind, you see..."

"Don't apologize. After all, we had no idea we were going to lose touch with Ron. Well, since we're stranded, we may as well reckon out what we have. I mean we might be wandering in the desert for days—people do—and there're so many wrong courses we can take! Let's do what Robinson Crusoe did and make an inventory of our stuff."

We did so; it helped to pass the time, for we did not wish to move away from that spot immediately, in case Ron returned to find us.

The completed inventory read as follows:

One truck.

Two ten-gallon containers petrol.

Water for two days.

One packet of hard biscuits.

Much equipment for excavating.

One pair Orange and Green pyjamas (Alan's).

One bar milk chocolate.

Two packets of cigarettes.

One exceedingly naughty photograph purchased in Cairo (Alan's).

Four pocket handkerchiefs.

The clothes we stood up in.

And one penknife, with instrument for extracting nails and stones (Alan's).

In addition to the above, Alan produced from the back of the truck a small case of lager beer, which he had put there personally as being an essential item to any desert caravan. Over a lager each we sat down and weighed things up.

128

The penknife wouldn't help us much, although Alan pointed out it would have been invaluable had we had horses, and had there been stones in the desert, and had our horses, if we had had them, chanced to get stones in their hooves, if there had been any stones in the desert!

The naughty photograph, although quite intriguing and a useful decoration for a bachelor's bedroom, was of no immediate use.

The cigarettes we lit up and smoked nervously.

The milk chocolate we ate.

The orange and green pyjamas had been ruined by the storm.

The packet of hard biscuits were too hard to be of assistance.

The water was, of course, invaluable, and so was the truck and petrol reserve.

So there it was. Our total worldly wealth, apart from a small amount of Egyptian money in our pockets.

We waited patiently until the sun was sinking in the sky. Then, having abandoned all hope of Ron coming back, we scrambled into the truck and set off to reach Farafra again before nightfall.

We had gone only a mile or so when the engine stopped and, on glancing at the petrol gauge, I saw we were out of gas. We climbed down again and forked one of the ten-gallon drums from the back. I thought it a little strange that we should be out of juice so soon, for the tanks fitted to the lorry were made to contain enough petrol to see us over about five hundred miles; and we had by no means covered that distance as yet.

But a further shock was in store. For the moment we laid hands on the ten-gallon reserve container we knew beyond doubt that it was empty!

And so was the second one! Now we were stranded with a vengeance, and we gazed at each other helplessly.

"But these containers were supposed to be full!" Alan exclaimed.

"I know that. But seemingly they've been tampered with. After all, the truck was standing overnight, you know, and someone could have got at them, I suppose."

Alan shook his head sadly and said: "And whoever did that also ran off the juice in the truck!"

We were certainly in a nasty spot. If we started to walk we might fail to hit any Oasis or sign of human being; the chance that we would choose a route which would take us back to Farafra or on to El-Bawiti or to any other smaller oasis, was about a hundred to one. If we failed, we should go staggering on into the heart of the Libyan desert, and would undeniably perish of thirst, hunger, or exposure to the virulent sun. Hundreds of miles to the Libyan border and then still desert for hundreds of miles more.

We talked it over at length and decided not to move any further for that day. Perhaps after we had slept we should be lucky enough to start our trek and stumble on a friendly, wandering tribe. Possibly we might stumble on a distinctly unfriendly one; there are bands of Bedouins and Tuaregs roaming the desert, tribes who would quite cheerfully slit our throats for the clothes we wore. In that event we had one item which we had not included in our inventory: an accurate revolver each and a supply of cartridges.

We lay on the tailboard of the truck and nibbled at hard biscuits, speaking but little. We had been lying there for two hours by Alan's wristwatch, when on the top of a dune some distance away a robed horseman became visible.

We could distinguish very little of the figure, but we stood on the roof of the truck and fired one shot each from our revolvers to attract attention. There was always the chance that the rider was merely the advance scout of a band of hostile

Arabs, but we had to take that chance, for unless we obtained help, we were almost surely doomed to perish in the desert.

The figure saw us. We saw it wheel its horse about and shade its eyes with a hand; for a moment or so it was motionless, and we were afraid we should be ignored. Then it turned in our direction and, goading the steed into action, plunged down a dune out of sight.

We waited breathlessly and could have cheered when the form of the rider mounted the next dune in our direction. It was now evident that we had been observed and that the lone horseman was coming along to investigate.

It was perhaps half an hour before the figure was sufficiently near to be recognizable; and then a gasp left us both, for there was little doubt that the rider, whom we had taken to be a man, was actually a woman!

She was heavily veiled so that we could not distinguish her features, about which the top of her robe was drawn to protect her skin from the sun and sand. But as she drew up and dismounted the robe fell aside and, beneath the burnous she had assumed, was the face of the dancing girl of Asyut!

I amazed Alan by performing introductions: "This is a young lady from Asyut—my friend, Alan Glenhaven."

"Delighted," stuttered Alan. "I see my friend knows you!"

"He has cause to," she smiled slowly. "I met him the night before you left Asyut, when I had reason to pay him a little visit at your hotel."

I caught Alan's admonitory eye looking at me and said hastily: "The young lady came to warn me that it would be dangerous for us to ride into the desert to the tomb."

"Of course. Now you find that I was right, do you not? Since you seem to be stranded here, I take it something has happened?"

"Something certainly has!" In a few words I explained to her what had occurred, and when I mentioned the empty petrol drums she nodded thoughtfully.

"I see! And now you have lost your friend and the map!"

"Unfortunately, yes. We hoped you would be able to lead us out of this mess!"

"I can lead you, yes. Possibly your friend has gone on to the tomb itself, eh?"

"It's possible. It may be that he thinks we will try to make for there ourselves."

"I think, then, it will be best if we try the tomb before we think about getting you back to Farafra Oasis. The Oasis is nearly fifty miles from here, but the tomb is merely thirteen or fourteen. And if you were going the direction the nose of the truck is pointing to you would not have reached any signs of civilization for at least one thousand miles!"

"There you are, you ass," said Alan to me. "I told you we were going in the wrong direction, but you wouldn't listen!"

"Why, which direction did you wish to take?" asked the girl with a smile.

"That one," said Alan, pointing to the left.

"Hmm! If you had had your way, my friend, you wouldn't have touched anything for one thousand five hundred miles!"

I said: "Before we start for the Tomb, tell me one thing: who are you?"

"I don't see why you shouldn't know now," smiled the girl. "My name is Lyria Wallef, of the C.N.I.B."

CHAPTER 10

BLOOD ON THE DESERT

A member of the C.N.I.B.!

Alan was looking puzzled, but I remembered Ron telling me the details about the Central Narcotics Intelligence Bureau, which is directed from Cairo Police Headquarters and has branches in Alexandria, Port Said, Suez, Tanta and Asyut itself. He told me much about the unceasing war which the Bureau, directed by Russell Pasha, wages against the drug traffickers, who seek to introduce opium and hashish into Egypt for distribution among the natives, whose use of Nile water causes a dire stomach complaint, which, in addition to sapping their manhood, is extremely painful. Drugs bring relief to these sufferers, and at the risk of injury to their health, they persist in taking them in large quantities.

"So you're a special agent?" I said. "But why the dancing? Why the role of dancing girl in a cheap café?"

"It's a long story—I'll tell you as we ride, if you wish."

"As you ride," said Alan, "I'm afraid we'll have to walk."

"It started when you reported the mysterious efforts to stop you reopening the excavations at the tomb of Ko Len Tep," said Lyria, as we commenced ploughing our way through the sand. "There had been a terrible increase in the quantity of hashish smuggled into Egypt, and the bureau was extremely worried. We thought at first that it was coming from Syria, and camel patrols ranged the desert to prevent the traffickers importing it.

"But one of our agents discovered that the central distribution point was actually under our noses in Asyut! We managed to effect one or two arrests, but we were unable to find out where the drug came from, or where headquarters were. We were certain that somewhere there must be a huge supply dump, and it was this we were very anxious to trace.

"When all the trouble about your excavations started, the bureau wondered if the attempts to stop you going to the tomb could mean that that was the dump. They had arrested certain Arab dancing girls from Asyut, and so they determined to put one of their own spies there and find out where the girls had obtained the drugs, which they were conveying on their wanderings to other villages.

"I volunteered for the job. I won't say it was very pleasant stripping myself, but it had to be done if I was going to find out anything at all. Certainly, they would never have expected any official agent to go to that length in her efforts to dig out the whys and wherefores of the game.

"I obtained the job easily at the Inn of the Sun by telling the proprietor that I had recently been dancing in Cairo, but that the police were on my trail for dealing in drugs, and that I had had to make myself scarce. He believed me, and it wasn't many days after I had taken up my job at the Inn when I was approached by him and asked to carry drugs. I accepted the offer, and worked for the gang until I was further in their confidence and had found out a lot more concerning their activities.

"It appeared that the ringleader was known only to a few; he lived in Cairo and was a respected man. I also learned that he was coming down to Asyut personally, to take care of the three English fools who were set on opening the Tomb where the drugs are stored!

"So now you understand, gentlemen, why it was imperative to certain parties that you did not open that tomb again. Now you know why Professor Glenhaven met his death there. Had he managed to penetrate through that inner door into the burial chamber he would have found not gold and jewels and gems, but endless quantities of hashish! The drug is stored in the tomb after being brought across the desert by wandering Arab tribes. Then, Arabs from Asyut go out and pick it up, bring it back to the inns and taverns, where it is given to the dancing girls to take with them to the next village.

"Now that we knew all this, we could have raided the tomb and the Inns. But we were anxious to catch the leader, and if he had been aware that his organization was wiped out, he could have skipped out of the country. Perhaps we wouldn't even have found out his identity!

"So we decided to let you gentlemen go ahead, and to keep our eyes open for our man. However, I found out that night you were at the Inn what the leader's plans for dealing with you were. It seems that he was even now in Asyut and was to some extent in your confidence. I only overheard the gist of the plot, but it was clear that he intended to strand you two in the desert, after having emptied your tanks of petrol, and to take away the other truck and your companion, with the map locating the Tomb. He considered that if he left the map with you two you might have been able to have another go at finding the tomb, whereas if you had no map, it would have been almost hopeless. He planned to work it so that it would appear as if the other truck, with the six workmen, who were really members of the gang, and your friend, had been lost in the desert! When I heard this, I felt I had to warn you, even at the risk of confusing the whole thing. I did warn you! But it made no difference; you went on with your plans!"

"It's hardly believable," I exclaimed. "It's like some plot out of a novel!"

"Almost everything in Egypt is," she smiled. "The Sphinx, the Pyramids, the Temple at Karnak; who could believe the wonder of these things without actually witnessing them!"

"And the blind beggar you spoke to this morning?"

"Merely another agent. The ulcers and hard skin on his face are a mask. Being thought a leper gives him greater freedom of movement and attaches no suspicion to him. When you saw me speaking to him, I was giving him final details of what was to happen. It seems that the first truck, after leaving you behind, was to proceed straight to the tomb. Meanwhile, a squad of swift racing camels, bearing a drug patrol is racing towards the spot in order to trap the leader himself, if he is there. Perhaps they have already arrived; I, too, was riding out to witness the final arrests. It was lucky for you that I decided to do so!"

"But, Ron," I gasped, realizing for the first time what a terrible danger my friend was in. "What will they do to him?"

The girl was silent, and her face expressed worry. She said: "We can only hope the camel squad arrive in time..."

After that we redoubled our efforts, and, lurching along in the sand behind Lyria, covered the miles with a quite astonishing speed. At last, tired and weary, we stood upon the top of a high dune, gazing down into a deep wadi.

For some time past we had been able to hear rifle fire, and now, circling about the other truck, which stood far down the wadi, we could see men mounted on camels and wielding rifles with great skill. Their hands never touched the reins; they circled at incredible speed, rifles in position at their shoulders, firing at the inside of the truck, where someone invisible to us must have taken cover.

"Those are our men," nodded Lyria, in answer to the question in my eyes, "but whether they have saved your friend or not is hard to say!"

Gradually the firing died away down there, and as we drew near the mounted men baited their camels and dismounted.

It was a grim, unpleasant scene which we came upon. All about the truck the sand was dyed with blood; figures, some wounded and moaning, some to moan no more, were sprawled upon the sand and half out of the truck itself. As we came to a halt, the Narcotic Squad, who had sustained only one casualty owing to the erratic aim of the natives, were sorting the dead from the wounded. Out of the six natives who had started the journey with us, only two remained alive, and these were seriously injured. Of Ron and Mahmud there was no sign!

A handsome, smiling officer alighted from a camel and came over. "This is your blind leper," smiled Lyria, as he spoke to us. "Mr. Gilmour is very anxious about his friend who was in the truck. Have you any news of him?"

The man shook his head regretfully. "I am afraid not. Nor have we succeeded in capturing the leader. When we drew near, these fools opened fire on us, and when the fight was over there they lay, dead or dying, and of the two who live neither will say a word."

"Have you examined the tomb itself?"

"Thoroughly. We found the drug, stacks of it, wrapped in two layers of rubber and packed in water-and-air-tight cans. In the inner chamber, the door of which was open, it seems that the cave-in, which was arranged to dispose of Professor Glenhaven, has since been repaired by the gang. I am about to send some of my men out to search the surrounding district in case our man has slipped the net. I will also instruct them to look for your friend."

"Do you mind if we look in the Tomb?" queried Lyria.

"Not at all. But I am afraid you will find nothing there. The place is bare, except for an old sarcophagus."

"Come," Lyria said, "we will try our luck in the tomb. Perhaps they have overlooked some clue!"

The entrance to the place was nothing more than a block of sandstone poised upon two side blocks of the same stone. But then a passage ran into the hillock of sand and we trod along it slowly, our way lit by the glow from Alan's cigarette lighter. After a ten-yard walk, we emerged into the outer chamber. It was not so gloomy here, for from a small opened stone door on the left came the flickering rays of a lamp or candle.

It was a lamp, as we found when we had entered. It cast ghostly rays upon the painted carvings on the walls, and pierced the gloom to reveal a long, wooden coffin lying in a hollow block of stone by the far wall.

The sarcophagus of Ko Len Tep!

But we viewed it gloomily, and without much interest, for the thought of Ron had driven all else from our minds.

Starting by the door, we commenced a methodical search of the chamber, but all it contained, besides the sarcophagus, were the drugs the officer had spoken of.

A sudden exclamation from Lyria made us abandon our search and join her by the sarcophagus. "Look!" she breathed. "The lid—it's been opened recently!"

Within a second we had thrown the lid off—and then, with shocked, horrified eyes, we stood petrified, staring down at the grisly object which was revealed!

Lyria gave a shuddering sob and turned away, face in hands, the failure of her mission setting in.

Alan's eyes were strained and anguished; his fists clenched and unclenched by his sides.

As for myself, my entire sense of feeling was numbed by the occupant of that ghastly casket!

It was Ron who lay there—Ron, whom we had found. But I would rather have never seen him again, than have seen him as I did, lying in that ancient box in a pool of his own blood, his throat severed from ear to ear and the bloody weapon of murder, in the shape of a curved sword, lying across his breast!

All eternity was crowded into those few seconds when we stood, pale faced, across the body of our murdered, mangled friend.

Alan's eyes met mine, and in both was an unbreakable resolve to know no rest until we had, in turn, murdered the foul wretch who had done this thing! He slowly removed his jacket and laid it gently over that ghastly dead face. The tension snapped with this action, and he muttered: "Poor Ron! I had a feeling something like this would happen—and it's my fault—all my fault!"

"Don't be a fool, Alan," I said, gripping his shoulders. "It isn't anybody's fault except the man who swung that scimitar! He's the only one responsible and he's the one who'll answer for it, if it takes me the remainder of my life to find him!"

"Me, too," said Alan. "This is one thing I'll want to settle with my own hands! The murderous swine..."

Lyria came over, averting her eyes from the silent form in the inner sarcophagus. She said, with a break in her voice: "I'm sorry. Perhaps it's my fault more than anyone's. When I warned you, I ought to have mentioned their plan to separate you. But I didn't know anything like this would happen, and I wasn't really supposed to mention anything to you at all. I'm sorry!"

In the gloom of that two-thousand-year-old burial chamber, I said slowly:

"Don't reproach yourself, Lyria! As I said, no one's to blame but the murderer himself! We agreed to see this thing through to the end, and we all knew what we were going in to. We had our eyes pretty wide open after what happened in Cairo. And if you hadn't been working on the case, the same thing would have happened! Obviously, Ron had to die."

"And it's a certainty that if they killed Ron, they also murdered poor Mahmud," she said. "Perhaps they killed him back in the desert and dropped him off the truck."

"They've a lot to answer for," I said bitterly. "But I say again, that if it takes the remainder of my life, I'll find and kill the man responsible!"

"It won't take you that long, Mister Gilmour," sneered a harsh voice behind us – and spinning round, we beheld the missing Mahmud!

139

CHAPTER 11

THE SCIMITAR OF JUSTICE!

Mahmud!

He stood there in an opened doorway, where formerly there had appeared to be nothing but a blank wall. A secret chamber! In his hand he held Ron's revolver. His hair was tousled and disarranged, but his hand was steady and unwavering. Upon his face was a sneer as he surveyed us; Alan without his jacket, fists clenched, face pale; myself, standing behind the startled Lyria.

"Kindly throw any weapons you have aside," he said, and as we made no move to obey, he repeated sharply: "Your weapons! I saw Everest hand you revolvers when we started this expedition. Unless you drop them, I shall shoot the woman!"

I dropped mine; there was little else I could do. Alan, minus his jacket, patted his trousers' pockets to indicate he was weaponless.

But the Dragoman's eyes had detected the coat which covered the dead Ron, and he snapped: "I presume the revolver is in the jacket? Kindly remove it and throw it towards me!"

Alan bent over, took the revolver from his jacket. He spun round and unexpectedly took a snap shot at the dragoman.

At the same instant, Mahmud's own gun barked, and Alan grunted and clapped a hand to his head. Then, slowly he crumpled and slid towards the floor.

Lyria took a menacing step forward while Mahmud was briefly fixated on Alan's figure, but I pulled her back. She'd never clear the distance.

"The fool!" sneered Mahmud. "Those shots will have told your precious Camel Squad that there is trouble here! Release your hold on the girl and let her swing shut the door leading to the outside—quickly!"

Lyria glanced at me, but I could only nod to her to do as directed. Mahmud had proved he was not afraid to shoot, and I had still a wild hope of turning the tables on him before he could do any damage.

Lyria swung the door shut, just as hurrying steps made themselves heard along the tunnel.

"Thank you," rasped Mahmud. "They will be unable to operate that door without considerable trouble. The mechanism for operating it is not very easily found!"

"What do you plan to do with us?" I asked. "You are trapped yourself, and it can do you no good to harm us. It will only add to the list of charges against you!"

"Does that matter, Mister Gilmour? I can only hang once, can I not? And first I have a score to settle with you and this lady and your friend on the floor, whom my bullet merely stunned."

"You intend to—kill us?"

"Certainly. But before I do so, I will let you into a little secret! You know me as Mahmud, the dragoman, brother of Mustapha the Dragoman! That, however, is far from being my real identity. My name, Mister Gilmour, is one you know well. You have dined with me once, in Cairo; that was when I first learned that nothing would cure you of your determination to open the tomb, and when I first decided you would each have to die!"

"You mean...you are."

"Arnold Selidan, at your service! The woman you followed that night in Cairo was my wife. I was the man who thrashed you as a preliminary warning, which, unfortunately for you, failed to take any effect! My wife helps me to run this drug business of mine. She is really exceedingly helpful, and is also very fond of the luxuries which the money we make will buy.

141

"Surely, you didn't think we could have afforded to live at Shepheard's on the meagre salary which the firm pays me? Really, Mister Gilmour, I had thought, having been a lawyer, you would have been more astute than that!"

"So you murdered Mustapha..."

"Correct. And died my hair and skin and altered my facial appearance by the aid of one or two nose plugs and cheek plugs. I pride myself that you had no idea who I was as Mahmud!"

"I see. Those reserve petrol tanks were never full at all. They were empty when you had them loaded, and you took care to put only enough juice in the tanks under the truck to see us well out into the desert, and no further!"

"That's it, exactly. I had planned to knock your friend senseless and drive off and leave you to flounder. The sandstorm, I regret to say, was not part of my arrangements—but it was very convenient just the same. Under cover of it I was able to overpower your friend and drive away. I brought him down here and...well,"—he chuckled—"you can see for yourself what happens to those who interfere!

"Yes, I am aware the game is up! But here I have the three remaining persons who are directly responsible for my downfall. Yourself, your friend, and this woman police agent. A pity I shall have to kill her, for I dislike harming women. However...as a member of the C.N.I.B., I can hardly pass on the opportunity..."

I leaned back against the sarcophagus, casually, watching Selidan carefully all this time. And now, as the unconscious Alan stirred and groaned, his eyes momentarily flickered towards the floor...I'd had enough!

My hand slid backwards and gripped the scimitar. I shouldered Lyria aside and hurled myself forward, and felt his shot into my shoulder, but then I was on him, and the force of my charge hurled him backwards into the secret chamber he had just left.

We fought it out there; a grim life and death struggle, and more than once my heart was in my mouth, as, braving the pain of my shattered shoulder, I strove to keep his revolver away from me.

He fired wildly, and I counted the shots as they ricocheted about the small chamber. Then the hammer fell with a feeble click! He was out of ammunition, and immediately I threw myself back into the other chamber and scrambled to my feet. He came out at me, his mouth frothing white, his eyes like the eyes of a wild animal, his fingers forming claws. Lost to all sense of danger, he came snarlingly onward. I stepped back a pace, gauged my distance, and caught unawares, I slammed my back achingly into edge of the sarcophagus. Sensing victory, Selidan rushed forward, when suddenly, a dark form latched onto his legs.

Lyria!

Halted by her manoeuvre, he paused to shake her lose. It was the only moment I required.

I swung the scimitar high, round, above my head... With every ounce of muscle in my good shoulder, I brought it round again, downwards, in a wide, curving sweep. I felt the steel bite against his neck with a force which almost threw me from my feet... I heard his sudden, hopeless screech as he felt the bite of the cold steel... And then the stroke was through, and the razor-keen edge sheered with demoniacal force through flesh, bone and muscle alike!

Selidan's head suddenly flew into the air, splattering blood over that chamber of horror. It thudded sickeningly to the floor beside Alan.

My numbed gaze fell on the results of my handiwork; the beheaded trunk; the raw, bleeding neck with the pipes torn and ripped asunder. The body tottered for a moment, its clawed hands feebly moving. It took a step, blindly, towards Lyria, and she shrank back with a cry of fear. Then it toppled stiffly floorward, where it lay still twitching convulsively.

For a moment, I was appalled at what I had done; then I became aware of Alan, who had staggered to his feet with the blood running down his face. His hand sought my arm—my good arm, thankfully—and his quiet voice said, simply: "Good man, Tony! That's for Ron!"

I became aware of a hammering on the door of the tomb. The Camel Squad. But it was a long time before they found the means of getting into the chamber; a long time, during which Selidan's detruncated head glared wildly from glazing eyes.

In the inner chamber from which Selidan had appeared, we found much of the stuff which had originally been buried with Ko Len Tep—stuff which Selidan must have been hiding for himself. Even then, I couldn't resist the chance of sliding one or two articles into my pocket. The Egyptian Government, I thought, would have enough not to miss a trinket or two!

While we waited for the door to be opened, Lyria bandaged Alan's head with a piece torn from her burnous. And then we sat and waited. Patiently.

CHAPTER 12

IN WHICH I LEAVE YOU

We attended the trial of Mrs. Selidan about a month later, at a mixed tribunal in Cairo. She escaped the charge of being an accessory to murder but went to prison for ten years on the count of having trafficked in illicit drugs.

I was glad, in a way, that they did not hang her. There had been too much bloodshed for my liking.

Lyria was there; I had been seeing quite a lot of her since we had returned to Cairo (at the tribunal) and intended to see a lot more. I told her so, and she smilingly remarked: "Hmm! I think you've seen quite enough of me already!"

"How do you mean," I said, indignantly, "I've seen enough of you?"

"When I did that Seven Veils Dance in the Kahn El Shems!" she retorted, mischievously.

I left the courtroom with Alan, who, having got over poor Ron's death to some extent, was more or less cheerful again. "Well," he exclaimed, as we stood outside, "I'm damned if I think so much of Egypt...not after it's taken poor Ron from us!"

We both fell silent while we remembered Ron and his tanned face, broad figure and cheery good-humoured conversation and erudition. I think there was a lump in Alan's throat. I know there was in mine.

Lyria called on me at my hotel later, for she had a matter to discuss which concerned us both. "I've given up the department," she said.

I nodded and said: "It really isn't any game for a woman."

"What is a game for a woman?" she asked, her eyes twinkling again.

"Perhaps I'll let you know, shortly," I grinned, and pulling her to me, I pressed my lips against her fragrant hair.

145

We clung to each other for some time, and I lost myself in the touch of her warm, pulsating figure, and the deep depths of her dark, shining eyes.

We were still embracing when Alan strolled in, without knocking, and began: "Tony, I want... Oh! Sorry! Didn't know you had Lyria! How? When?" he blurted. "Certainly not at the Tomb!"

"Heck no. Lyria came to see me at the hospital when the bullet was being extracted from my shoulder. Things sort of developed…"

Rolling his eyes, he turned to leave.

"It's all right, Alan," I called, as Lyria gave me a final kiss, "come right in!"

"Some guys have all the blessed luck," snorted Alan, eyeing me enviously. Lyria laughed and ruffled his hair.

"Want anything in particular?" I demanded.

"Eh? Just—well, I wanted to ask your opinion about this little knick-knack I've picked up from a trader..." He extended towards me a small, circular piece of clay. I took it curiously and examined it. It was about four inches in diameter, red coloured, and curved like a saucer.

I said: "What the devil is it?"

Alan flushed a little, and glanced at Lyria, who was gazing on with interest. "I gave him five hundred piastres for it. It belonged, he told me, to none other than little old Cleopatra. He said it was one side of Cleopatra's brassiere!"

Lyria burst into a ripple of laughter.

"And he charged you five hundred piastres?"

Alan nodded. "He also said he'd try and get me the other half at the same price!"

"You're priceless," laughed Lyria. "You've paid all that money for a cooking pot made out of clay, as used by the people of the Lower Nile!"

"A—a cooking pot?" gasped Alan.

"Nothing but!"

A wrathful expression appeared on Alan's countenance. He turned a deep red. "Damnation! I'll get that scoundrel, you mark my words!"

He flew out of the room, going at a good speed, leaving the late Cleopatra's brassiere lying on the table. I looked at it idly and said: "I bet Cleo was a strange woman! Look at the things she did to the chaps who loved her!"

"Why think about that?" said Lyria, softly: "or are you tying me up in your mind with her? Perhaps you're afraid of me?"

I couldn't let that pass, could I? So, drawing her toward me again, I proved I wasn't!

THE END

Other books in the Vintage Crime Library series
published by Williams & Whiting

Mr Budd Novelettes Volume One by Gerald Verner
A Case For Dr Morelle by Ernest Dudley
When Shall I Sleep Again? By Norman Firth
Mr Budd Novelettes Volume Two by Gerald Verner
Dr Morelle Meets Murder by Ernest Dudley
Spotlight on Norman Firth Volume One
Mr Budd Novelettes Volume Three by Gerald Verner
Dr Morelle's Casebook by Ernest Dudley
The Little Grey Man by Norman Firth
Mr Budd Novelettes Volume Four by Gerald Verner
Send For Dr Morelle by Ernest Dudley
The Model Murders by Norman Firth
Mr Budd Novelettes Volume Five by Gerald Verner
Dr Morelle Elucidates by Ernest Dudley